Quentin S. Crisp

HAMSTER DAM

Quentin S. Crisp was born in 1972, in North Devon, U.K. He studied Japanese at Durham University and graduated in 2000. He has had fiction published by Tartarus Press, PS Publishing, Eibonvale Press and others.

quentin s. crisp

HAMSTER DAM

THIS IS A SNUGGLY BOOK

ISBN: 978-1-64525-083-8

HAMSTER DAM

"With it shall go this record of mine—this test of my
own sanity . . ."
—H.P. Lovecraft, 'The Call of Cthulhu'

the stories makes me think we don't quite realise how big the change has been in the last hundred years. It's like a huge, secret change. You can't pin it down to a time or a place, and no one's even given it a name."

"What do you mean? Does he write about this change?"

"No, it's not that. For instance, the last one I read, 'The Green Room', I felt like I had to slow down to read it, like I'd arrived on another mental world, and I had to get used to thinking with different gravity. You know, he was a pretty popular writer, but his paragraphs are like something chiselled out of stone. Pretty much no one in the world has the time to explore this kind of detailed mental landscape anymore."

He paused as if he considered he had somehow failed to make his intended point.

"Anyway, so that's how I've been spending my time," he said, and lapsed into silence again.

As this reading matter seemed a fruitful topic, I tried to question Gary further, but I was puzzled to find that, despite his initial burst of enthusiastic eloquence he was reluctant to discuss the stories or their author at any length. After a while, I had the impression that Gary's mind was elsewhere, as if the silence of the flat was a music to which he was listening. As I would have if he'd actually been listening to music, I became quiet, in order to share his listening.

Eventually, he smiled to himself and sighed. He got up, took the book from me, walked over to the dining table again, and pulled out an old wooden drawer from the space beneath the tabletop. I detected in his movements a consciousness that he was watched coupled with the knowledge—uncertainly held but defiantly asserted—that he could do as he wished in his own flat. When he returned to his armchair and I saw what he'd taken from the drawer, I thought I understood, though there were fascinating subtleties in his action. From a small and intricately carved wooden box on his lap, he drew out tobacco, cigarette papers, a lighter, and a lump of hashish about the size of four sugar cubes. He proceeded to roll a joint. This was hardly a novel sight and yet I felt constrained to silence, as if to speak now were somehow to interrupt. Once the joint was rolled, the paper at the smoking end twisted up in a sort of fuse and ready to light, and the discomfort of the long silence was quite palpable, Gary stood up, disabled the smoke alarm on the ceiling, looked at me with a sharp, inquiring expression, sat back down again and struck a flame from his lighter.

"Self-reporting, eh?" he said after exhaling a long cloud of smoke from deep in his lungs. "Self-reporting . . . ?" He seemed to be searching through a directory in his mind under this entry. "How about this?" he proposed; "I hate *The Big Bang Theory.*"

With this statement and another prodigious inhalation and exhalation of smoke, he extended the spliff, between his index and middle finger, in my direction.

I hesitated and sighed, yet my hand had already moved in the midst of my hesitation. Perhaps only I had been aware of this hesitation, like a slight resistance in changing gears. I felt, somehow, that I had given in. As I brought the joint to my lips, I naturally crossed my

Gary winced visibly. "Is that a neutral comment?"

"Maybe."

"Nice." He passed the joint back to me with a raised eyebrow. "Well, maybe I have been doing a lot of thinking, yeah. I was thinking about the way I used to be, as a child. I didn't, you know, as a child, think that boys shouldn't like butterflies and flowers and pretty things. All that came later. You know what the Tate Modern kind of artists would say about a carving of a butterfly? If it wasn't obviously ironic, they'd call it sentimental. You see what I'm saying?"

He scrutinised my face and I realised he was waiting for a reply.

"Yes, I think so," I conceded.

His eyes dropped now and he seemed to be considering something.

"Do you remember that children's TV programme?" he asked at last, as if, after everything else, he had finally got to the one thing he really wished to speak of. "Hamster Dam?"

"Hamster Dam?"

"Yeah." He smiled, but there was uncertainty in his eyes. "You remember, right?" He paused again. "Must have been seventies, or early eighties. There was a whole village of hamsters, with windmills and tulips and so on, and the main hamster used to fly a biplane. You must remember."

I shook my head.

"It's not ringing any bells."

"That's so strange," he said. "I never hear anyone talk about it."

"Are you sure you're not making it up?"

"No. How could I make up something like that? I remember it."

"Have you tried looking on the internet?"

He made a pained expression and seemed to shake his head a little.

"You don't remember it then?" he asked again.

"I'm afraid not."

He stared into space, reflectively, as if letting something go—watching a boat disappear over the horizon.

For some reason this turn in the conversation made me uncomfortable. It felt maudlin. I thought some kind of stimulation might facilitate a change of subject and I looked around for Gary's Nintendo console. I realised that this was one of the subtle differences in the environment of the flat; the console would usually have been in front of the television, but now I couldn't find it.

"Where's your Nintendo?" I asked.

Gary appeared to take a breath before replying.

"I've put it away," he said. "I was going to sell it, but I don't even want to pass it on. It was the Nintendo that was the last straw. That's why I've been going for walks and reading Walter de la Mare and playing music and staying offline."

"Why? What do you mean?"

"It was the ad for the new Zelda, actually. Somehow it just struck me as insult to injury. They know exactly how to crush your spirit and that's what they enjoy doing, with their bare feet. It's like your broken spirit is the courtyard, however, I accepted the reality of the night as belonging to that of the air I breathed. Only, because of the strangeness of time's flow as I had experienced it, and the Indra's web of inner and outer worlds, I now saw this darkness of night as somehow containing the brightness of the day it had succeeded. The door closed behind me, but I was in no hurry. I stood at the concrete wall forming the edge of the gallery and examined its scaly, grey cactus hide. I stroked it with my fingers, and looked down below, at the central raised square of garden in the courtyard. It was like some ingenious puzzle of angled leaves. I had a sense of enclosure, and the words came to me, "This is the well of time." Protected. Deep. Still. Away from the world of days and demands that I knew. Another world, somehow represented in those leaves, as if they were the very shape to fit the lock that stopped all time. I sighed in satisfaction.

Eventually, I moved on and left the housing block behind. The night was warm and I knew if I missed the next train there would be others. There had been thunder at one point earlier in the day, and some of the walls I passed glistened with damp in the light of streetlamps. I had no particular desire to arrive anywhere and I thought of what Gary had said of his recent walks. The world was already here, and people forever passed it by, looking the other way. I came to a path with trees on one side, running parallel to the train tracks, which were, at present, silent. On the other side of the path was a thin strip of waste ground, bordered by a wall half obscured with the growth of ivy, bramble, valerian and so on. I stopped here, on the path, alone, finding something wonderful in the idea that in all the world only I was conscious at this moment of this exact location. My breathing became one with my listening and watching, as if it was the perceptible extension of space that I breathed. I thought I heard a rustle amid the overgrown grasses—perhaps of a mouse or other rodent. I was aware of a soundless sound beneath this, as if I could hear the thickening fibres of the vegetation itself, the very sound of its life. It was a sound infinitely deep, infinitely layered.

I stood there, wishing I could become rooted in that sound. At last there began, in the distance, the building rumble of an approaching train. After the evening I'd had with Gary, and in the mixture of urban street lighting and moonlight, the entire scene had more than a trace of the strange, reptilian quality I'd found in the Rimewell Estate, but the thickening fibres of that soundless undersound were so naturally attractive to me, so easily bypassing, in their appeal, the reservations and preoccupations of a lifetime, that I made a determined mental note to return to this spot in daylight.

■

I suppose I needed a pretext, for my own sake—a rationale at least vaguely professional—for visiting Gary at the weekend. There was nothing to stop me visiting socially, but it was important to me to maintain the idea of a professional structure to my visits. As things currently stood, it would be all too easy to blur the boundary between professional relationship and friendship, which was, after all, the same kind of mistake that Gary had made. I am sure—almost sure—the desire to visit came first. Then I told myself that I had detected signs of especial vulnerability in Gary on that first visit and that he needed to feel someone was on his side, not that he was simply being examined. The desire that preceded, or accompanied, this apparently rational decision was the desire to taste again that drifting timelessness that had become rarer and rarer in adult life. All the conditions of Gary's flat were conducive to this, and the weekend would augment them further. There was nothing irregular in my actions, narcotics aside. I could easily dispense, in this record, with some of the above remarks if my only desire was to justify myself, but that is not my purpose.

So, the Saturday immediately following the first visit, described above, I made my second visit, this one from early afternoon. My impressions of the first visit had remained compelling and I did not forget to stop, on my way from the station to Rimewell Estate, in that place of leafy neglect where I had experienced the soundless sound.

The strangeness of the night had gone, or, more accurately, it had transformed into a tranquil, less intrusive strangeness. I listened, trying to sound the nuances and the extent of the daylight soundlessness. A lizard skittered across a bald section of the wall, from one patch of leaves to another. The stillness expanded bottomlessly. Nameless life thickened and flowed in a harmony of generation and disintegration. I felt an obscure satisfaction, as if, in this way, I had succeeded in making an appropriate frame for my second visit to Gary.

Before I talk about that second visit in any detail, I must give some background as to why Gary was taking leave from work. Some of this is a matter of record, anyway, so that my motivation for giving my own account is slightly undermined, but some information is always privileged over other information in the degree of attention it receives, and people always underestimate how much interpretation adds to fact. Besides, I think there is some matter on this subject that has not been known outside of a very limited circle of consciousness, sometimes confined to Gary and myself. Needless to say, there must also be plenty I don't know. And also, there is more than one circle of consciousness, and some circles are less permeable than others. For which circle or circles am I writing this? At the moment, the smaller and fewer the better, but I would like this truth to exist in some form I can believe is safe.

Just over two years ago, a client was admitted to Crane Hill House, having been sectioned after a psychotic episode accompanied by incidents of self-harm and apparently credible threats of violence to neighbours. Her name was Julie Wilcox. She was thirty-two years old, though she often looked at least half a decade younger, and her biography was cratered with the ravages of emotionally unstable personality disorder. I mention her appearance because there was unmistakably a rare kind of glamour about her. It was as if she were both the victim and the beneficiary of her own vampirism. Or to be less neatly symbolic, it was as if the self-harm that made her haggard also, at certain times or at the right angle, also proved to have been an uncannily youth-preserving beauty regime. For this reason alone, it would not have been surprising for Julie to attract Gary's attention, but there were other reasons that, knowing Gary as I do, I believe to have been more important in the long run. For instance, although her celebrity did not exactly precede her, it slipped in with her like a gust of unseasonal wind from outside. It became known, once she was with us, that she wrote poems and other 'things'—more or less unclassifiable—and that she had even been published. Some of her writings were viewable on various poetry websites with names like lImInaL, CuntRa and VerSus. In fact, few of us were more than momentarily interested in this information and I think only three or four of us took the trouble to read anything she'd written. I was one of this small minority and Gary was another. From the very beginning, Gary expressed an unusual degree of admiration for Julie's poetry, but I was sceptical—both of the poetry and of Gary's admiration. It was not that I thought he was being consciously deceitful. My impression was more that he wanted to admire the poems and had the imaginative resources to be able to project upon them a spangle of nuance and enigma to compensate for the consistency of inner vision and literary style that they lacked. To do both Gary and Julie justice, his enthusiasm almost convinced me, in both the above senses, more than once. Her poetry, even if I discounted Gary's influence on my judgement, was at least better than average for the venues that published her, some of which were exclusive enough to demand payment from the reader. She was something of a name on the slam poetry scene, in particular, and on this score I felt very little scepticism. On one occasion, in Crane Hill House, I saw her perform. The audience was limited to myself and Gary. My prejudice concerning performance poetry is that no one involved really wants to be in the audience; they merely suffer this in patience because they are there by accident or they hope to take their turn, sooner or later, at the microphone. It's a kind of joyless and sterile incest. If you, as an audience member, find to your surprise that this or that poet was not entirely painful, you can give an acceptably convincing impression of having enjoyed their work, thus perpetuating the general pretence that the scene is worthwhile. Julie didn't exactly persuade me otherwise. I could see the—predictable—influence of rap in what she did, forcing me to suspend judgement, since I have never had a feel for the genre. I could also see she had something of the savvy for meme-like presentation that is common among those who have grown up with the internet. In other words, I understood that she had a respectable packaging that she had worked at, as one might work at a dance routine. It was not accidentally embarrassing, though it did make me uncomfortable.

Aside from the rather grudging and negative praise I have just given, I found the rap-doggerel of the words teetered on the brink of real acuity. The poem was called 'Match-Girl', the title signalling some gymnastic wordplay that just about landed on its feet. 'Match'

her request would, paradoxically, be to demonstrate in a small but distinct way, that she was different. But he knew this already, which was why he hesitated. So, he accepted her request for two reasons: Deliberately in order not to treat her differently, and, under cover of that, because he wanted to. As he did so, he told me, he felt a small but undeniable "fuzziness", which he tried to forget as quickly as he could.

I am not sure that anyone knows the exact correlation between Gary's relationship with Julie and Julie's death. There is at least some, in my opinion, but partly in a way for which I must share the burden of responsibility. Julie had been on suicide watch when she had first been admitted, but gradually—perceptibly—she began to uncurl from the ball of foetal self-destruction that had characterised her attitude and appearance at the beginning. This was also a factor in my restraint vis-à-vis Gary's very visible closeness to her. Eventually, when reviewing the question of security surrounding Julie, I consulted Gary, informally, before the formal process took place, asking his opinion on how safe it would be to allow her freedom during the day. I told myself beforehand that in this way I could, at the same time, also subtly probe Gary as to the nature of his attachment to her, but when it came to it I did very little probing and satisfied myself with a gut feeling of reassurance. In any case, Gary insisted that Julie was no immediate danger to herself or anyone else, and suggested that allowing her to take part in poetry slams would be very good for her rehabilitation. He said exactly the same thing in the formal meeting. I had already fallen under the influence of Gary's point of view from our off-record conversation and it's possible that in some subtle way we presented a confident united front to the others involved. The decision was made in favour of relaxing security and allowing Julie occasional days out.

There is another way in which I suspect there to be a correlation between Gary's attachment to Julie and her death. I have never previously made this thought explicit to anyone, though the suspicion will not be surprising to any who have much experience working in mental health. The suspicion is this: that Gary was in many ways an opportunity for Julie. Was it a case of 'transference'? Whether or not that would be an apt diagnosis, it is hard for me to resist the impression that he was to her an emotional and dramatic sounding board. He was an apt enabler, almost uncannily suited to her needs. Maybe he sensed this, almost in confusion, and took it for a thing of beauty. She, on the other hand, was perhaps first brought up short—a little affronted even—and then, understanding the situation, becoming sure of it, grew agitated with an excess of exhilaration. If I were intending to make this document public, I would no doubt hesitate to write what I have just written. Public morals are all too often a matter of maintaining appearances, which means that it is necessary to be seen to be shocked by certain ideas. For the sake of such appearances, examples are made of dispensable individuals. It is easier to do this than to explain the messy realities of any given situation to the public. What messy realities? For now, I think it will suffice to put the matter as follows. Most people are, in their default attitude towards others, trusting. They will have a strong inner resistance to thinking that a person might be lying to them. On the one hand, such distrust seems like a grave and even a demeaning accusation. On the other hand, at a slightly lower level of consciousness, there is a deep fear of stepping into a sinister world in which others are always to be suspected of evil designs. It is a good thing that most people are like this, or the world would be in an even worse shape than it is, but it is questionable how realistic this default position is. I know of at least two groups of people who do not operate with this default position: the police and those who work in mental health. But I should return to my narrative.

Gary was mentioned in a few of Julie's last poems. One even gave his full name. I suppose this might be considered the poetry of particulars, or some such thing, but I am not convinced. The poet "does not count the stripes of the lily", supposedly, but Julie kept a very public tally of stripes in this case. I believe the purpose was other than poetical—it had more to do with theatre, and even more to do, I cannot help but think, with an irrational but cunning desire for revenge. In that poem there was a line, lacking scansion but arresting nonetheless, that declared: "For me you stole temazepam from the drug trolley." Questioned on this as part of a delayed internal investigation, after a referral for formal investigation had been sent to the Nursing and Midwifery Council, Gary insisted the line was a metaphor and that "I never gave her anything she wasn't prescribed." I rather think that, true or false, the intention of the line was literal; if false, he was making the futile gesture of protecting her by avoiding saying that it was a lie. If true it would be a serious matter, but the internal investigation found no evidence. As for the NMC, in the end, the hearing never took place.

Julie performed this poem and two more mentioning Gary on the night of her final poetry slam. Gary was present on that occasion. She left the venue by stealth before the event was over, was missing for three days, and was finally found in a canal, drowned. There was a frightening mixture of drugs still in her stomach when her body was examined, indicating either suicide or misadventure. However, even before her body had been found, suicide was feared, and not only because of her track record. Between her disappearance from the poetry event and the discovery of her body, she wrote a series of hysterical and incoherent messages on Gary's Facebook wall. They were a potent brew. There were accusations, but when the identity of the accused was not veiled, the exact nature of the accusation was, so that one way or the other they were difficult to counter. To attempt to counter them, in fact, would have looked like guilt, but knowing Julie as I did, I detected some jaw-dropping lies in the mix—that is, lies if one completed the implications made. And then, amid the kind of babble that a third party might believe could make sense if only one knew the full story, there were occasional deadly stabs of what appeared to be pointed lucidity. One message was simply the following: "You knew what game you were playing from the start. I'm the truth about your life that you couldn't stay away from."

Gary was, as he told me, tremblingly aware that any attempt to defend himself would be seen as 'blaming the victim', since it would be a foregone conclusion in certain quarters that she was 'the victim'—that is, even before they knew what the situation was in which that was her—inevitable—role. Therefore, he responded to the messages on the wall briefly, asking her where she was and why she was upset, and trying to reassure her that all the help she needed was waiting for her. He sent her longer private messages, but she reposted these to his Facebook wall, mocking their content viciously, and he decided he had no choice but to deactivate his account. Soon after this, of course, we learnt the final fate of Julie Wilcox, though what had immediately preceded it remains, even now, an eerie blank.

Needless to say, the whole thing affected Gary very badly. Even if there had been no suspicion of misconduct, he would have needed to take leave. On the one hand, he said these events had the brute impact of sudden pressure, but on the other hand there was something subtle and precise about them. The pressure had located the hidden fault line of his flawed personality and forced a crack. He pictured it like a tidal wave shuddering against a glass barrier. The wave is a monster, but it can squeeze its way through the tiniest of cracks, forcing them wider and wider until everything shatters and is swept away.

As yet, the barriers still held inside him, but he had felt the crack. He reverted, then, to that word, "fuzzy". He had felt the fuzziness in a tiny thing—the acceptance of a friend request—and he had been right. It had spread like an apocalypse of white noise, and now joined him, with nightmarish ambiguity, to the death of a young woman. Gary went as far as to anatomise the fuzziness to me soon after Julie's death. First of all, in his own words, though he did not consider himself a predator, he could see he was not "angelically innocent". It was hard to measure one's own shortfall where innocence was concerned, but this was entirely the point. Second, to explain was to "protest too much" and to accuse oneself was slyly to "deflect blame". Third, to keep silent was merely to protect one's own guilt. These were the basic elements of the fuzziness.

I found myself vacillating between two undesirable poles: affirming his own pessimistic view of the situation or minimising his feelings by offering the perspective that training and experience bring. Perhaps it would have been easier for me if I had not begun to feel fuzzy myself.

When a small group of protestors demonstrated outside Crane Hill House with placards about "the patriarchy" and sexual abuse (at least one of them, "Oedipus got it half right", was reasonably witty), it was the third element of fuzziness, as he saw it, into which Gary lapsed. I was exasperated. The protestors were singled out for ridicule and abuse by some obsessives among the red pill community online, and in some quarters, of course, this put the seal on their righteousness.

■

him how to use the money. Eventually, he'd built a huge machine, according to their instructions—something that looked like a kind of spooky tanning bed. He used the machine on himself and the voices became clearer and clearer until he began to see the creatures who were talking to him. They were these little midget-like alien things with massive heads that lived in another dimension.

"Now he could see them, and hear them clearly enough, they began to explain to him what the whole reason was they'd been telling him to do all these things. They wanted him to make thousands of the machines so that he could begin to treat the whole human race with them, so that more and more people would be able to hear and see the creatures.

"I've thought about this a lot lately, and I think there's something important about this bit. In a way, it's this bit that proves it's a great story. It has a weird, ambiguous effect based on something that's not said. It's never revealed what the ultimate purpose of the creatures is. They want humans to hear and see them, and it's absolutely essential that this happens, maybe for the fulfilment of the human race, or to avert some catastrophe, or for some other reason. I suppose as a child I imagined that it was something like . . . Actually, I don't want to put it into words. The point is, there was a question in my mind as to whether the creatures should be trusted, and because the story itself never posed the question, that doubt affected me quite powerfully. I had to weigh it up. I mean, I was really serious. Can they be trusted? They look weird and a bit scary, and

God only knows what they actually are! Or maybe even God doesn't know. Maybe that's exactly how spooky they are. But I weighed this all up, and I decided, like the hero of the story, to trust the creatures, almost . . . maybe exactly because I thought the value of trust itself made that the right answer.

"But to get back to the story, one thing I forgot to mention was the fact that Bill was married. Naturally, his wife wanted to know what was going on, and eventually he had to explain to her, as it looked like it was his life's work, anyway. So he told her everything—how the voices started, how it was because of them that he'd found all the treasure, how they'd instructed him to build the machine, and how he could see the midget-things now as clearly as he could see her, and was talking to them all the time about his mission to make more of the machines.

"Naturally, this freaked her out a bit. She started crying. Then she got angry. It was at this point I always got a horrible sinking feeling reading this comic strip. I knew that there was no talking to her and that she wasn't going to let things be. And she doesn't. She talks to the family doctor and her husband is basically taken away in a van. He screams and resists and is told it's for his own good.

"Somehow, there's this psychiatrist with a machine that is effectively the opposite of the machine that the man built for himself. Bill's strapped into the machine and given a series of treatments. Gradually the creatures fade from his vision and their voices become inaudible.

"I'm not sure what happens to the machine he

built. Maybe it gets smashed or something. Of course, he'd never be allowed to use it again, anyway. So, his doctor is very satisfied, and his wife says, 'I'm so happy you're back to your old self again,' and so on. And he kind of noncommittally says, 'Yes. I'm sorry I went off the rails. I must have been crazy.' The first time I read it, I thought, 'Is that it? Has he forgotten the trust he placed in the creatures?' That would have been a horrible ending, too, but it's not quite like that. In the last panel, you see him walking down the street, arm in arm with his wife. She's quite happy, smiling and chattering away about normal, daily things. But you can see he's frowning and there's a faraway look in his eyes. He's thinking, 'I wonder what happened to them. I can't hear a thing anymore.' But you, the reader, can still see them. They're right in front of him, saying, 'Bill, Bill, can you hear us? Bill, Bill, you've got to listen. Please, Bill, listen to us!' . . . And that's the end of the story."

Gary was quiet now and watched me intently, as if he was determined not to be the first to break the silence.

"Well, that's interesting in a lot of ways," I said. "But do you think the psychiatrist in the story represents all psychiatrists?"

Gary shook his head and held up his hand as if to stop me.

"I think," he said, "we should save interpretations till later. I want to tell you . . . about Hamster Dam."

"Hamster Dam?"

"The children's TV programme, remember? I mentioned it last time."

"Oh. Oh yes. I remember. What about it?"

"I've been dreaming about it."

He kept a strange, steady gaze on me as he spoke and after he lapsed into silence.

"What kind of dreams?"

"Confused dreams, to begin with. Or at least, I couldn't remember them properly when I woke up. I'd already dreamt of Hamster Dam half a dozen times before you last visited. Do you ever get recurring dreams, by the way?"

"No. Not since I was a teenager."

"I've never had recurring dreams before. Not that I remember. Also, these seem to be recurring by theme but not repeating the same incidents. Except, some sequences are repeated."

"What sequences?"

"Mainly the opening titles."

"Opening titles?"

"Yes, of the TV show. That seems to be how I get there. I can't explain it, exactly, but I think that's how I arrive at Hamster Dam. The opening titles are a kind of . . . interface."

"Alright, so tell me about the opening titles."

"Well, fairly standard for the seventies—white lettering scrolling down the screen over scene-setting pictures of Hamster Dam. It's very simple stuff. But there's something I can't describe. You see a tiny model narrowboat floating down a sparkling river between banks of piled moss, and the camera goes upstream and there are windmills, red, yellow and blue, with their sails turning slowly, and a little, furry hamster face, with bright, beady eyes, pokes out of the top window of one of the windmills, and then you see the same hamster pegging clothes up on a washing line. She looks really real. I mean, not like a puppet, but like a real hamster hanging out the washing. Then you see that the line is strung between two windmills on either side of the river, both of them surrounded by red and yellow tulips, and the windmills and the washing line act as a frame for the whole village of Hamster Dam, which is now visible, rising up to the horizon, higgledy-piggledy.

"It's a bit hard just to come out and say this, but it's like some kind of rodent Shangri-La. I mean it's . . . perfect."

Gary stopped, sighed and raised his eyebrows as if reassessing the task of dream narration that he'd set himself.

"I see all this in the dream," he said, resuming his task, apparently having decided he had no choice but to continue. "But I should give a bit of background here before I go further.

"The main character in Hamster Dam is called Blue Boy and is actually a guinea pig, which is a bit confusing, but this guinea pig almost doesn't fit in. He's like a trickster, always upsetting things, accidentally—probably—but then this is also part of his personality."

"Ah, wait a minute," I said. "Blue Boy? That is ringing bells somehow . . . No, it's not coming back to me."

Gary nodded.

"*The High Chaparral*?" he asked.

"*The High Chaparral. The High Chaparral.*" I repeated the title to myself. "Yes. That's it. I remember, but . . ."

"Yes, there was a character called Blue Boy in *The High Chaparral*, too, which is also a bit confusing. What's even weirder is the fact that this guinea pig dresses like another character in *The High Chaparral*: not Blue Boy but Buck Cannon. He wears a kind of black leather cowboy jacket, and I swear his facial features are somehow the same, even though he's a guinea pig and the other Blue Boy, I mean, Buck Cannon, is human. He has the same eyes, too. They're definitely the same eyes."

"Wait, don't you think this means—"

Gary waved his hand again, then put both hands, one inside the other, to his mouth, in contemplation.

"Sooooo," he said at last, "where was I? So . . . yes . . . Blue Boy. You get this idyllic scene-setting of the title sequence, and this revelation of Hamster Dam between the two windmills, then you hear the sound of an engine and a wailing voice, always saying the same kind of thing, like, 'Who put that windmill in the waaaaaaaay?' Like that. And then Mrs Van Poggle, the hamster we've just seen, will scream out something like, 'Oh, Blue Boy, not again! My washing! My washing!' and Blue Boy will go, 'Aaaaaaaaaargh!' and his biplane—because he's flying, of course, really badly and recklessly—will go twisting and twirling about and will snag Mrs van Poggle's washing line and tear it away from between the two windmills and will crash-land, breaking one of its wings, on the bank of the river. Then you'll see him emerge from the wreckage, blinking, with his flying goggles pulled back, and his facial fur a bit sooty, and he'll say something like, 'Ooh er! Just as I thought!

Left wing needs reinforcing.' That kind of thing. Then the title sequence will fade to black and the individual episode will begin."

"But don't you think," I said, taking advantage of a pause, "that this is something you've made up somehow? Literally dreamed up, I mean, rather than remembered."

"Well, that's the question, yes, but it's more complicated than you think. I need to tell you about the dream first, then maybe you'll see.

"As I said, I don't remember that much from the first few dreams, apart from the opening titles, and what I do remember is just impressions and images. The titles somehow took me into the world of Hamster Dam, and there I'd find myself in the wreckage of Blue Boy's biplane with him, as if I'd been his passenger. After that, each time, I would be in the village of Hamster Dam. There were gardens full of flowers, and amazing food, as if I was eating real food for the first time, and windows looking out from cosy kitchens. It's the feeling more than anything that stays with me."

"What feeling is that?"

"Happiness. Don't you think it's strange that I can experience greater happiness while asleep than I ever have in my whole life while I'm awake? It's not even just more happiness, it's as if I know what happiness is for the first time, as if I've been living in a world where people don't even know how to imagine happiness and suddenly I'm in a world where the real thing is normal and everyday. It's almost eerie to have the last shadow of doubt removed."

"You begin to suspect precisely the lack of doubt?"

"Well . . . I'm coming to that. I remember eating some kind of seed cake and looking at a real geranium in an earthenware pot and being completely free of anxiety. Indescribable!

"Anyway, maybe we can talk more about that later. The thing is, after you last visited, there was a kind of breakthrough. I remembered more when I woke up. Also, I'm pretty sure the content of the dream was different, and there was a different quality to it, like lucid dreaming. The dream was commenting on itself."

"What did it say?"

I could see now that Gary was settling in to relate the real substance of the dream and perhaps of everything he had hinted at so far. He shifted in his seat as if for greater stability and bowed his head, pausing for quite some time before he continued.

"I was taken into the Dam itself. The Dam is located in the foothills of the mountains, miles back from the village of Hamster Dam. There's no time to talk about the workings of the Dam. Anyway, there's a huge, rotating, live-in staff of hamsters maintaining the place, and you can feel the vibration of the hydraulics the whole time. But it's more than what we understand as a dam. Blue Boy took me to one of the highest chambers in the whole construction. The process of getting there was strange. I'm going to have to cut a lot out. I'll start with the antechamber. I was sitting alone in this grey, concrete antechamber. It was empty except for a bench built into the wall, and there was a window—an aperture, really, without glass or anything—just under the ceiling in the wall at a right angle to the bench, and a big slab of a door, like something inside a pyramid, opposite that. Light was streaming through the aperture. The light itself was refreshing. It made me feel transparent. I remember thinking that the window was like a port to receive things from the open sky. I knew I was really high up and that I was waiting for something. I was literally at a threshold, but I also had a sense of what that meant, more than at any other time in my life. That was what I was meant to feel in that place. Even waiting there, I knew something was happening.

"The door slid back and a voice called me from the next chamber. I got up from the bench and stepped over the threshold and Blue Boy was sitting there in the corner on a tasselled floor cushion. He was wearing his usual black jacket, but also a bandana. He looked different somehow. It wasn't just the bandana. Whenever I looked at him it was as if my vision was in close-up. I could tell that he wasn't quite made of the same reality as human beings. There was something about him like the stop-go animation of *Bagpuss* and all those programmes, but he also seemed really warm and alive.

"On another cushion in front of him was one of those Tibetan singing bowls, and in front of this was another floor cushion. He told me to sit down, and I did. Then he picked up a little stick from next to the bowl and hit it. It was like feeling the opposite of a whirlpool inside me—an expanding outward spiral. It felt like I was going to melt completely. Then he looked at me and spoke. I was really scared, in the dream, that I would wake up and forget his words, because I knew they were the most precious thing I'd ever heard. But somehow—thank God—I think I've remembered them all. It went like this:

"'You are wondering how something so unreal can be so real. I'll tell you. Hamster Dam is a Between Thing and those are the things that truly last forever. Only the Between Things can be infinite. We exist in a vibration: on, off, on, off, on, off. You can remember it as the Alternating Current.'

"He hit the bowl again.

"'Like this vibration. You have to tune in, and then you are part of it. To tune in, you only have to tune all of the wrong things out.'

"For a while he didn't talk and just hit the bowl at intervals. Each time he hit it it was as if the sound became a little bit sweeter, a little bit purer. Then he carried on.

"'On. Off. Because we were off, when we're on we're more real than real. Off. On. Because we were on, when we are off you wonder where we went. This is what you hear in the sound of this bowl.'

"And he went on hitting the bowl. After a long time I felt I had to ask him a question and I said, 'What do I have to tune out?'

"He said: 'There is something that degrades the vibration. We call it Direct Current, but sometimes, also, we call it Digital Cancer. It doesn't turn off. On on on on, without any gaps. It kills all Between Things. Your world is infected with it now.'

"He kept on hitting the bowl and it got sweeter and sweeter, but I was horrified because I could hear and feel, in the innermost part of me, exactly what could be lost. After a while, I asked another question: 'What is the Direct Current?'

"'You know what it is. W.W.W. On on on on on. Everything on on on until nothing is ever more real than real again. Soon, on your world, Direct Current will lock in and there will be no escape. It is only the Between that can help you. You must be careful. Dream at the right time. Wake at the right time. Make something known so others can escape; but keep something secret or the door will close and there will be nowhere anymore to escape to. That is the whole knowledge: Make something known and keep something secret.'

"Then he stopped hitting the bowl and stood up. I felt incredibly refreshed, but also as if I'd just received the burden of a vast responsibility. That's just it, though—responsive. That's how I felt. Anyway, he led me over to the glassless window in the far wall to show me the view. I could see the curve of the Dam's wall, with sparkling streams of water running down it, and here and there were other windows or apertures like this and occasionally a furry hamster snout would poke out. The sky was a pale blue and it looked like it went on forever. The river below rolled away through woodland and pasture to the village. Everything seemed clean and pure and real. It was like a promise. And then Blue Boy said, 'We'll meet again,' and that's the last thing I remember before waking up."

There was no mistaking how powerfully this dream had affected Gary. Moreover, it was apparent that he had made himself vulnerable in telling me about it. The last thing I wanted to do, therefore, was to frighten him into withdrawal by making any ill-considered judgements. If I was right, this dream, and what it represented, could be the necessary key to Gary's rehabilitation. The line it seemed most prudent for me to take, with all this in mind, was to ask Gary what his own theories were concerning the existence of Hamster Dam as a real television programme and the nature of the dream's relation to it if it did exist. I questioned him, for instance, on whether he had found anything about the programme online. The question seemed to put him on edge, and I wondered if this had been a misstep.

"Yes. Yes, I did try doing a search. This was one of the weird things, finding nothing on the entire internet when the memory was so real to me. The title itself has been used, but not for a children's TV show. There's an episode of The Wire called 'Hamsterdam', without a gap between 'Hamster' and 'Dam'. I've watched it. No clues there. But there's also an obscure self-published book written by a boy when he was ten. That's a bit more interesting. I ordered a copy. I'll lend it to you before you go if you like.

"Apart from that, the title doesn't even crop up, on the entire internet. The thing is, this is part of what Blue Boy was talking about. It's the Between Things that are important. I've remembered Hamster Dam now I need to because it's a Between Thing, and the fact that it's not on the internet is one sign of this.

"I've thought about this a lot since we last spoke and I'd like to ask you to keep it a secret."

"What, Hamster Dam?"

"Yes."

"Okay. Fine."

"And don't look it up."

"Why not?"

"I'd feel much happier if you didn't. You don't have to, do you?"

"No, I suppose I don't. Okay, I won't look it up."

We talked at some length and I will include some of the content of this talk in my generalised summary of Hamster Dam as Gary related it to me.

Again, we smoked. Gary played the guitar, and I was aware of two apparently contrasting feelings that achieved a strange harmony: that I was sharing a precarious and deluded psychic space with Gary; that I was idling with him in a kind of cosmic rusticity.

Before I left that day, Gary retrieved the book he had mentioned from his bedroom. Standing and looking aimlessly about the flat, I saw a sheet of paper containing the lyrics Gary had been singing when I first arrived. The title was 'The Discovery of the World'. I recognised it as one of Julie's poems.

IV: The Dream Horde and the Grove

That he remembered it and that it was real, that was what made Hamster Dam so inexpressibly important to Gary. Obviously there was some question about the meaning of the word 'real' in this context. Gary himself was unceasingly aware of this question, as if the question were a fountain of water and he were a ball balanced, revolving, at its apex. The nature of this reality, he told me, came before the question of whether Hamster Dam was real simply by existing in this world or not. The kind of real he was talking about, he said, straining for words and at last finding an approximate term, was *meta-real*.

Because of the dreams, however, which he now had without fail when he slept, as if to dream was by definition to dream of Hamster Dam, he did not have to rely on ineffable abstractions to communicate to me the nature of Hamster Dam. The dreams were an unfolding cosmological map. Over the next few visits, I attempted to piece together with Gary the fragments of that map. I will try to reproduce here, in words, as much of that map as is needed for my account of events and—I hope—as will convey at least something of the emotion that Hamster Dam inexhaustibly inspired in Gary. It is

a difficult task for many reasons and I won't be sorry
to leave off from it as soon as I can, since the emotions
that it now inspires in me are something like those of
poring over a map of Atlantis after having watched it
sink beneath the waves.

Hamster Dam did not have a beginning as such—
not in a temporal sense—though it might have had
an inception. One dream contained what seemed an
anomalous image. Hundreds of hamsters were zorbing
across nebula-festooned interstellar space, each ham-
ster-containing capsule trailing a tail of fire and cosmic
dust, like a comet. The hamsters were as if ejected from
some old and dying world in search of a new one, and
the dream showed them making landfall, emerging
with twitching whiskers from their zorbing balls in
craters made by those craft on eerie wilderness plains of
primitive vegetation.

The relation of this scene to Hamster Dam itself was
never specified in any way that Gary could remember in
waking life. However, he retained enough information,
as well as impressions attached to no particular images,
to make some broad surmises. Hamster Dam was time-
less but not ultimate. The scene of intergalactic zorbing
might have represented something like the inception of
Hamster Dam, but when Hamster Dam was cultivated
it did not spread in a single temporal direction from
past to future. Instead, it spread like the leaves of a dan-
delion, along the ground in all directions.

There were techniques involved in the cultivation of
Hamster Dam that were entirely outside the bounds of
human science. In fact, it was hard to say whether they

were science at all according to the current human understanding of the word. The conceptual structure and value system underlying the techniques were entirely different. 'Progress' was not considered anything more than a relative value, dependent on context. Progress towards what? was the question, and since in Hamster Dam they already considered they had arrived at their destination, all progress thereafter was to do with organic growth, general nurturing and refinement of what already existed.

This was not in the least monotonous, Gary explained, because, as if tending the most beautiful of gardens, the rodents of Hamster Dam had perfected means of accommodating the growth of various contradictory sequences of events sideways and otherwise tangentially in time, like pathways among hedges, fountains and flowerbeds that diverged and once more converged, diverged and converged, the intersections always redolent of the enigma of time-flux.

One of the secrets of Hamster Dam was to be discovered in the contemplation of such intersections, since, as Blue Boy had said, it was only because of the Between Things that anything mattered or could ever matter. Some places in the human world, for reasons that were hard to explain, had more of the Between about them than others—and some *times*. But it also required that a person become attuned before this was apparent. Someone who was especially well attuned might see varying degrees of time-flux in the everyday objects of a room. Time-flux was not the Between itself, but was like the ripples where one body of water meets another, or like the splintering of light that occurs when the declining sun shines from behind a balustrade—a symptom of the Between, in other words. Even those who could not see it, however, might sometimes be astounded by the strangeness and mystery of an object without being able to give a single articulate reason why—this shop window at dusk, or that sagging garden gate, or a coat discarded on the arm of a sofa.

In the human world, Between Things had been especially prevalent in the 1970s, at least among those decades still within living memory. This was why, despite its timelessness, Hamster Dam was rooted in that decade. So many secrets like this were explained to Gary in the course of his dreams that, piecing them together, he began to see the world around him with an entirely different perspective. 'Perspective' was the right word, he said, since that meant some things appearing smaller and some larger according to distance. In his analogy, he had gained a perspective which made some things appear suddenly in the foreground, as more important, that previously had been unnoticed in the background.

The appearance of Hamster Dam itself was liable to change. Usually it was the sun-blessed village of windmills and flowers, but sometimes this was replaced by a maze-like metropolis of globes and boxes connected by transparent tubes. It was not that one of these appearances was the reality and the other an illusion, although the former was the one Gary claimed to remember from his childhood—each needed the other, as a root needs a flower for propagation and fulfilment, and a flower needs a root for sustenance. The Dam itself, though, Gary believed, existed as some point of mediation between the two appearances, and it was for this reason that Blue Boy repeatedly took him to the Dam to explain what was necessary for him to know. He was more likely to remember what he was told in that place, or it was a little easier to explain things there in a way that would still make some kind of sense when he awoke.

Gary related a number of sessions that occurred in the same chamber in which Blue Boy had told him about Alternating Current. At one such session, Blue Boy had swapped the bandana for a headscarf and sat at a small, round table, draped with a red-patterned cloth, on which there sat a crystal ball. Blue Boy motioned with a paw for Gary to sit in the rickety wooden chair opposite him. When Gary did so, and peered into the light-spangled sphere over which Blue Boy made mysterious gestures with his paw, he saw a sequence of images unfold that, without words, conveyed a story.

The first image was a wooden walkway of duck-boards that crossed a river, with reeds growing at the walkway's edge. From between the reeds, two lustrous minks bounded onto the boards, followed by a third, gambolling and frisking together as if they were incapable of any movement that didn't have a life-affirming elastic springiness to it. In the intervals of their play, the mustelids stopped and looked about blithely. They were not tame, Gary realised, but their wildness was untouched by a fear of human beings.

The view inside the crystal ball swept over the surface of the planet. Human cities, which had come to resemble factories built around the production of the human commodity, had ceased to function, and slowly the Earth was shrugging off its mantle of concrete. Of humans themselves there was no sign. They had been discontinued long since.

"The minks shall inherit the Earth," pronounced Blue Boy. "The reign of Direct Current will come to an end, but humans will have been cannibalised by their creations long before then."

Gary understood the triumphant irony. The mink was an invasive species, crossing continents because it had been bred and slaughtered for its coat.

He asked Blue Boy if this would certainly come to pass.

"On the road ahead it is a certainty," said Blue Boy. "Only a turning to the side can avoid it."

But, as he confided in me, Gary did not believe that humanity would make that turning.

In another dream, Gary asked Blue Boy why he spoke so wisely and with such changed diction in the Dam when in the village he was a foolish rascal.

"This is the secret of love," said Blue Boy. "Very few humans understand it. Even your human gurus perpetuate a very great cruelty in this matter. The higher self loves the lower. The lower self is not an illusion. It is alive with the love of the higher self."

On yet another visit to that high, light-filled chamber in the Dam, Blue Boy, wearing a trilby, had prepared for Gary a sandbox full of toys—model cars, soldiers, plastic dinosaurs and so on. Gary recognised it in a rapturous upsurge of long-buried memory. When he was a child, there had been a friend of his parents, an old lady, who offered an unusual kind of therapy. She used a sandbox filled with all kinds of toys and objects she had collected. The person undergoing the therapy would arrange whatever objects they chose exactly as they wished in the sand, and then the old lady would ask them questions about whatever particular arrangement they had made. His parents had often lent her a room in the house for this purpose. Gary had been so deeply attracted to this activity that he would often sit outside the closed door of the room, hoping for glimpses of the sandbox and the enigmatic, sometimes frightening arrangements of objects made by the old woman's clients, and listening, without much understanding—even when he caught the words—to the slow, soothing murmur of the question and answer, which seemed always to be opening up—gently, gently—some sad, strange, wonderful secret.

Gary had never once been allowed to play with the sandbox, though he longed to. It would have felt like the magical granting of a wish if only he had once been indulged and treated as one of the old woman's clients. Instead, his parents had chided him and told him not to sit by the door of that room because it made the clients uncomfortable.

It was this sandbox that Blue Boy now presented to him.

"Do you know what this is?" asked Blue Boy.

"Yes," said Gary, and he nodded.

"Now the time has come," said Blue Boy. He waved his paw over the sandbox. "You are ready to obey your own will."

brought from the celestial beyond as they moaned through the carven instruments of ice, rock and bone that were grouped like weird statues around their harsh dens and burrows.

I can almost hear those winds myself now.

But perhaps, after all, I have said enough about Gary's dreams. Anything else can be explained as the narrative makes it necessary. At this point in the story, the most salient of the dreams are that in which the sandbox first appeared and a number of others in which Blue Boy elaborated on the significance of the sandbox.

These dreams indicated that Gary would soon find, in the waking, human world, what Blue Boy had referred to as "the turning". It was here that there would be a potential *way through*, an escape from Earth before Direct Current became "locked in", which it would do soon. This exit, however, could only be actualised by shared belief. Gary could achieve this in the way Blue Boy had taught him over the course of his dreams, but he must then establish that same link of belief with another human being. Then the tumblers of the lock would turn and click into place and the way would be made open, not for two, but for one. One must remain to find a different turning. In this way hope was to be kept alive.

One of the asymmetries indicated by time's arrow is that of hindsight. It is almost inconceivable to me now that I heard Gary's words on this subject and failed to register their implication, but then my ideas of what were possible and impossible, true and untrue, precious and without value, were quite different. I was unable then, because of a few trivial prejudices that ruled my life as they rule the lives of so many human beings, to act in the way that was so urgently required of me. I was unable even to begin to understand.

There was a place in the waking world, Blue Boy told Gary, that in some way corresponded to or coincided with a place in Hamster Dam. Blue Boy took him to that place as it existed in the dream world. They left the Dam by a very long flight of stairs that joined the outer wall of the Dam to the mountain that rose beyond it. Then they climbed a thin and often broken mountain trail. At last they arrived at the ruins of an old chapel, its stone walls collapsed in several places. There, Blue Boy indicated a number of things that Gary was especially to remember. There was a yew tree—he could even smell it, redolent of dust and sap, outstanding in its reality. Among the tumbled stones and little crabbed trees inside the wall, a four-legged creature hopped—a rodent with long ears. Blue Boy pointed to this, too. It seemed to Gary wild and magical in this context, oddly devoid of the anthropomorphism of Blue Boy and the other Hamster Dam rodents. Then Blue Boy pointed to a pole near the chapel itself, at the centre of which was a cylinder not unlike a reel of cotton in shape, but of a very dark wood, and carved on the outside with antique letters and ornamentation. Windmill blades at the top of the pole turned in the occasional wind, and then the cylinder revolved, too, with a faint rustling and rattling from inside. Gary recognised it as a form of prayer wheel.

"Silent voices," said Blue Boy.

"Why don't we go there and sit down and you can tell me," said Miriam.

Gary looked up at her. There was no hesitation in her expression. He nodded in agreement and they set off across the grounds.

They entered the bamboo grove and sat together on one of the benches facing the sandpit. There followed, said Gary, an extraordinary conversation. He told Miriam about the sandpit that had so fascinated him as a child. He did not let her know this, but at certain moments during the conversation he was almost convinced that she was the same woman to whom, in his childhood, his parents had lent that spare room for the purposes of the mesmerising sandpit therapy. He did not know why this impression should be so irresistible; she looked really quite different. After telling his story, he asked her if he might, for his own personal therapy, make use of the library's sandpit. She seemed happy enough to give this permission, but reminded him that ultimately it was not hers to give. Other authorities were deciding the fate of the library and its grounds. In any case, she would not interfere with him and she would try and warn him at what times it would be best not to be around. She added that she believed the library itself would approve that someone was making use of its grounds in such a way during this between time while it was doomed and yet not gone.

Gary, of course, especially noticed the use of the phrase "between time".

He began to ask her about the library. The council, she said, had decided to close it down, with the plan, it seemed, of converting it into a gym, perhaps renting some of its space out in other ways. The plans were not yet finalised, but the library qua library was already in disuse; what was clearest in all this was the motive to make some quick money from the expedient in one way or another. In fact, 'expedient' was hardly the right word—whether they would even save money in the end, let alone make it, seemed doubtful. She half believed that career politicians had an instinctive and unconscious antipathy towards culture. It was not 'useful' in their schemes, and therefore they distrusted it. She had been at the library for thirty years—on the one hand, an eternity, on the other, the blink of an eye. (Gary began to see that she had stories she wanted to tell, too.) Books had always been a secret haven, she said. She had learned over the years what kinds of people hated and sneered at the existence of such a haven. There was a certain kind of intellectual whose only real goal was superiority—these people, in the end, always hated books, since nearly anyone can share in the secret haven of the written word if they wish to. Similarly, there was a particular kind of puritan who always hated books, since books are too forgiving of human nature, too inclusive. And somehow, these types and others like them—the inverted snobs, for instance—had steered people, in recent decades, away from this haven. It was tragic that people had somehow been persuaded that books were their enemies. But now that this insidious trick on the human race had succeeded, there was nothing that could be done to counter it in terms of direct action. If one launched a counter-attack, it would only accelerate the general alienation between books and people. And for herself, she did not regret her life in the least, though it looked as if, in terms of the immediate and even the foreseeable future, she and others like her were on the losing side of history. No, she didn't regret it in the least, because the longer one spent immersed in the secret haven of books, the more one became aware of the subtleties of their infinitely varied relations, one to another. Those subtleties were a whole world, a vale in which to wander, an aromatic revelation, forever unfolding, of the unsuspected. It was, she said, in its best moments, like arriving in paradise and realising that all the depictions you had been shown of it were the most flavourless of stereotypes perpetrated by advertisers who had never been to the place they were advertising. "Yes, like arriving in paradise, afraid that you'll have to give up all those dear little subtleties of the soul, and then being served ginger beer in a flute glass by someone in a peacock mask. You take a sip and laugh, and breathe a sigh of relief. You realise paradise is not as ghastly as it's been made out to be."

She continued: "Of course, one has to know *how* to read in order to get this result. I don't just mean the alphabet, grammar and so forth. I mean that being a reader is as much a skill as being a writer. There's no shame at all in being a really good reader and not writing a word."

As the conversation continued, Gary settled into a feeling of security in Miriam's presence. He was no longer incredulous that she had listened to him. Maybe there had even been some subtext of understanding to their meeting in the first place.

And now the library was like fallow ground, said Miriam, but she sensed a kind of destiny in this. There were unguessed seeds buried here. Somehow it was part of the secret nature of the haven that it must ebb like this, and seem to disappear. Perhaps it was selfish, but she was more enchanted with the library than ever now that its future had been curtailed. Recent events were like an unassailable benediction, a strange fulfilment that she could not explain. The world was losing something, which was sad, but in some mysterious way, she felt deep down that she was gaining something. And somehow, it would not end with her.

They talked for a couple of hours or more. At the end of it, Gary gave her his e-mail address, in case she needed to get in touch with him. He did not ask for hers, but she "remembered", as she said, that she had a card, which she passed to him. "Please use the e-mail address at the bottom. Not the library one," she said.

Gary looked at the cheap business card with its copperplate script. "Miriam Harelock." Something struck him about the written name, but at first he could not think what it was. Then it flushed through to his conscious mind. It had not been a rabbit Blue Boy had shown him in the dream. Of course—it had been a hare!

He couldn't help smiling, but he tried not to grin and stare too stupidly. Did she know? It was safest, anyway, to assume not. He gathered himself to say something, though he was as yet uncertain what he would say. While he was still gathering himself, Miriam looked at her watch; she had to go. Would he mind leaving with her, she asked; she intended to lock the gate. It was only some time after he had started on his way back home that he remembered he had not found the bridge. Dreams were imperfect messengers, he thought, or perhaps, after all, it wasn't the place he was looking for. Anyway, he was glad he had found it. He could not wait to return. This time he looked up the public transport routes, visiting again the day after his initial discovery. In particular, he wanted to spend time at the sandpit, in what he now called "the Grove". He made a quick visit to a toy shop and bought a few items that appealed to him, then he proceeded to the site of the library. Although the encounter with Miriam the day before had lifted his spirits and coaxed to the forefront of his emotions a sense of expectant mystery, he was not especially keen to meet her again immediately. There were things for him to do, by himself, in the Grove, and he was impatient to begin. He did not tell me, at first, much of what he did in there, but I assume, with the newly bought toys, he tried some version of the therapy that had been the focus of his longings and wishes as a child. I suppose he could not go far in this first foray, but he had a pen and notepad with him and made notes for ideas on how to develop this strange project he had started.

While he was there, in the Grove, he occasionally paused to wonder at the stillness of the library grounds. With each repetition of this pause, the sense of some wordless mystery attaching to this place deepened in him. Eventually, he decided to head home and put the toys he had bought back in the bag from the shop.

He didn't start immediately for the gate, however, but found himself roaming the grounds again and moving in the general direction of the library building. His sense of enigma found no definite object, and after a little while he came to the library's front entrance, still locked, as he confirmed by testing. He saw no sign of Miriam, and the interior of the building, visible through the ground-floor windows, was as gloomy as it had been the day before. It was tempting to believe he had imagined the encounter with Miriam, but he knew this was not the case.

He walked to the left, along the paving at the edge of the wall, peering inside with greater intentness. Silent voices indeed, he thought. The massed codices on shelves, now undisturbed, except, perhaps, by the fingers of one Miriam Harelock, seemed in their neglect to take on a shadowy life. Did they hear each other, perhaps? Contemplating such things, Gary turned his attention idly to some notices that had been stuck in the window. They were the usual kind of thing, advertising events, services and so on in the local area. Someone was giving guitar lessons; there was a reading group meeting in the back room of a pub. Then his eye settled on a notice a little apart from the others, printed in a conspicuously amateur design of hands and playing cards with pink, blue and yellow ink, now very faded. Bridge. Did people still play bridge? Then he began to shudder. "Old bridge." He could hear Blue Boy's voice. Scouring the minimal information on the notice, he saw that the area code of the phone number was from the time before the codes had been revised. Why had this notice been allowed to stay here so long, though the others were clearly more recent?

Old bridge.

It was certainly what he had been seeking—what he had given up on. Now, in a paroxysm of fear, he turned and hurried from the grounds.

Once more, he told me, he had to ask himself whether he trusted the rodents of Hamster Dam. When he got home he lay on his bed awhile and shivered. His shivering continued for some time in such an automatic way that he began to wonder whether it was purely physiological. Was he merely cold? In the middle of summer? An English summer, mind you. Now he felt percolating up from the depths through his shivering, an at-first voiceless bubble of laughter. More of the bubbles began to surface and burst, now with voice. He laughed, helplessly, until he was quite weak. Yes, he thought, yes, of course he trusted the rodents of Hamster Dam. He felt warm again. What Blue Boy had promised was being fulfilled. It was only hard to believe after all the cruelty and, even worse, the neglect of the human world in which he had been born and raised. But as the laughter bubbled up those two words sank down deep within him: Old bridge. And the combination of this particular rising and this particular sinking was deep relief and soaring elation. He believed.

This was the story he told me. Its telling had an engulfing momentum to it that both compelled and disturbed me. The excitement of it was too far ahead of where I found myself—it stifled me. When Gary had finished telling me his tale, therefore, I found myself oddly anxious about the time.

"There's an easy way over the wall," said Gary, "even when the gate's shut. I could show you the Grove and you'll see for yourself what I'm talking about. I've made a real start in the sandpit now. It's just the beginning, but it's something."

I was not listening. I thought I was being merely reasonable. It was already late in the evening. It would be better for me to come another time and in daylight.

There was an immense barrier of contrast between Gary's intoxicated urgency and my trivial practicality—the barrier a symptom or cause of the contrast. Gary had not, until then, realised what was between us, how far we had diverged without my telling him—in short, that I was not with him.

V: Mental, Spoken, Written, Digital

I did google "Hamster Dam". Or rather, I was about to use Google and then, by some obscure impulse, decided to use one of those search engines that guarantee privacy. The results were as Gary described: one episode of *The Wire* with a similar title and the curious self-published book he had lent me, written by an eleven-year-old boy about the place that hamsters go to when they die. It had seemed ridiculous to me that I had been prohibited from verifying whether or not Gary's memory of Hamster Dam was shared by other human beings. Of course, not everything is on the internet, despite what some people claim, and so this was not finally conclusive. However, I was glad to have a certain measure of ambiguity removed. On the other hand, I had broken my promise to Gary.

The next time I saw Gary, after his tale of the Grove, he was somewhat subdued. I noticed a tone of irony in his speech that had not been there before and he had also returned to the weary reticence of two months previously, before he had told me in detail about Hamster Dam. He agreed to a graded return to work and spoke calmly about "getting back to normal" and the hope that the NMC hearing would pass without issue. He acted as if he was embarrassed about all he had told me in recent weeks, as if he no longer knew quite what he should say about it.

I asked him about the Grove.

He nodded in affirmation, it seemed, of the question itself, and I was glad of some signs of earnestness at last.

"Yeah, I'm still working on the sandpit," he said. "It really seems to be good therapy. Maybe we should do something like that at Crane Hill House."

"Maybe we should," I said.

I am not a regular reader of the local news, but having been professionally, as it were, the confessor whose job is to hear soul-secrets of a distressed section of society, I have developed a more than casual interest in what the press chooses to select as newsworthy concerning the larger population from which my smaller sample is drawn. For this reason, I do occasionally pick up a copy of the *Hinter Vale Bulletin* along with a copy of the *Guardian* at the supermarket newspaper shelves, telling myself that I am taking a reading of the area's psychic barometer.

Perhaps a week after talking to the newly reticent Gary, having visited him once or twice in the interim, I was at the supermarket again and saw quite an atten-tion-grabbing headline about a vigilante group who had delivered a paedophile to the police by luring him into a trap with promises of underage sex. I judged there would be a great deal of quite gamey psychic meat in that particular number of the newspaper, so slipped

"It doesn't look as if you're very good with secrets yourself," I called back.

After that there was silence until Gary returned with the tea and a plateful of biscuits. He retrieved his own tea from the kitchen and then sat down opposite me.

"Yeah, well, touché," he said, dunking a chocolate Rich Tea in his drink.

I had the sense that he needed time and so I waited.

"I know how it looks, Brian," he said at last. "I know how it looks. Every time I did that—spoke to someone like that on the street—I could feel myself hitting this invisible force field. Funny, I didn't feel that with you, but I was wrong. Well, never mind that. The point is . . . well, that is the point. I need to get someone on this side of the force field. I have to do it."

"Why?"

"I've already told you why. I've told you everything, pretty much."

There was a sadness in his voice I had not heard before.

"Imagine I'm stupid. Spell it out to me."

"You don't believe me," he said faintly. "It's like Blue Boy said. Someone has to believe me or I'm trapped. Trapped. And then all I have to decide is the size of the psychiatric ward I'm kept in."

I bowed my head. How could I answer this? To lie at this point would be disastrous.

"I want to believe," I began, searchingly.

"Do you? And throw away your work pension? I'm not even sure that I want to believe now. I suppose that's how it works. The safe road leads to nightmare. To find anything real we have to go through madness."

"Well, what do you want me to do?"

"I'm not asking you to do anything. Not now. You came of your own accord."

"I want to help you."

"Maybe this is it," Gary breathed out in despair. "Maybe I'm condemning myself till the end of time." He laughed strangely. "That's the easiest thing to do. God, help me. . . . All right, I'll show you. Maybe you'll understand, even if you can't actually believe it."

"Show me what? The Grove?"

"Actually, there's something else. I'm not good with secrets, remember?"

He went over to his work bench and turned on the computer at the far end. When he had connected to the internet he drew up a chair next to him and called me over. As I watched, he typed "Hamster Dam" into the Google search engine. The screen flashed up with the results and I saw that they were curiously changed since my search, but then, I hadn't used Google. This time, at the very head of the search items, was a link to a Hamster Dam website. Gary clicked on this.

"See?" he said.

I nodded, puzzled.

"When did this come online?"

"I don't know exactly. I hadn't done a search for a long time until recently."

"Gary, I have a confession. I know I said I wouldn't, but I did do a search, not long ago, and I didn't find this."

"I'm not sure I follow you, Gary."

He laughed, his tone somewhere between despair and derision. "No. You mustn't. But anyway, I shall drop some hints. Have you ever noticed that when you suddenly have an idea, make a discovery perhaps, and think you're original, suddenly it starts to mushroom here and there on the internet? Have you never had that?"

I nodded. "I have had that," I said.

"Yes. What do you suppose triggers it? Maybe an internet search wouldn't be quite so mysterious, but what if it's just speaking to someone about it? Or thinking about it? Do you think, perhaps—just perhaps—the person who made that website read that newspaper article?"

"Well, I—"

"This is probably just a flurry of confusion for you. I'll slow down. You felt it, didn't you, that strangeness in your voice?"

"Yes, I did."

"And what did you think of that website?"

"It was . . . very strange. Very . . ."

"You don't have to tell me. I'm just asking you to think about it for yourself."

"But what do you think is happening?"

"Direct Current. It's cutting off the escape route. You can see that, can't you?"

I nodded. Something had happened. I could see it.

And it was very odd—the more I thought about it, the odder it seemed—that those images on the website matched my imagination so exactly. Was this what was meant by 'between'? It had happened, but not everyone could remember it, or . . . I needed to get a better grasp of the whole thing. There was no denying I was involved. I had to go to the Grove with Gary and see what—

Just as these thoughts were expanding and unfolding in my mind, swelling to a crisis that would precipitate action, there came the hard, shivering sound of breaking glass. Giant hairy caterpillars of fear undulated up and down my body. After a moment I realised the sound had come from the kitchen. Gary had shot up from his seat and now stood immobile in the centre of the room as if sniffing for danger. The flat was permeated with a thickness of uncertainty. Cautiously, I also stood up and looked about for a hefty object of some sort.

Then the voices began. They weren't speaking, or shouting exactly. It was unclear what they were doing. Since the intentions behind the voices were a mystery and since there were no words, we were both stunned for a while, listening in horrified fascination. It seemed to be a chant, yet it was not a chant. There was a low, menacing, rhythmical stutter of three or four voices in unison, and then a wailing began in time with it, an ululation that seemed the prelude to the climax of some secret ceremony. I suppose it must have been only a few seconds, but after what seemed a ridiculously long time, the meaning of these sounds became clear. Gary and I exchanged glances. It was an a cappella and somewhat tuneless version of the theme music from Doctor Who.

I felt a quite particular sensation when I realised this, and I wonder if Gary felt the same. It was a temptation to laugh—a temptation as if it were an actual decision to be made. I wanted to laugh—for laughter to be the resolution of this scene—but just as I was about to, a doubt formed in my mind. It seemed to me that if I did laugh I might discover the reality that laughter had no place here, was banished. The attempt to laugh *with* might find itself without even the reassurance of being laughed *at*.

Now there came other voices.

"Paedophile!"

This was repeated a number of times and some strange noises followed of movements and of something falling in the kitchen. Gary rushed through and began swearing. Then he called me with a kind of intimate urgency. There was a fire in the kitchen sink. Something flammable had been dropped there. Beyond, through the windows, was the movement of figures hovering just out of view.

"I'm phoning the police," Gary called out at them. Then he turned to me. "Brian," he said, and pointed to the flames.

I loped over and gingerly, trying not to get burnt, I turned on the taps. Gary went in search of the phone he had switched off. I didn't want to stand too close to the broken window, but filled a saucepan at arm's length from one tap and then poured the contents over the remaining flames.

"Are you his bum boy, you dirty bastard?" one of the outer figures enquired.

There were other, similar taunts. I heard a neighbourhood door open somewhere, I thought, and a couple of windows, and heard them close again. Now I could hear Gary talking in the next room. He was giving his address. I looked around the kitchen. There seemed to be nothing of much use in a siege situation. Still attentive to the broken window I twisted the top off a pot of chilli powder. If one of the little thugs came near the window, they'd get it in the eyes. I considered the various kitchen knives but didn't like the idea of thrusting my arm through broken glass. Besides, even without this disadvantage, wielding a knife seemed like a bad idea.

I was beginning to think we had won the battle of nerves and was almost elated at the idea when I heard a ping and a whizz and felt something sting me in the left flank. An air pistol. I wondered if I was bleeding, but dared not check. I became suddenly afraid they would aim for the eyes.

Quite unexpectedly, as if he were peeping in to introduce himself, one of our tormentors showed his face at the broken window. The hood of his top was down and his features were visible. He had short, greasy-grey hair with a fringe cut straight across a forehead angry with spots.

"What are you looking at, paedo-beard?"

I was aware of a feeling, flushing poignantly through my physical pain, of outraged indignation, since he obviously wanted to be seen or he would not have put himself on show in this way.

"Fucking hell, what do you think you're doing with a paedo-beard like that?"

For some reason these questions were the most confounding riddles, and left me tongue-tied.

"He's borrowing it from a spastic, the dirty fucker," came a helpful voice from somewhere behind him.

At this point Gary returned to the kitchen.

"The police are on their way," he said, "so you'd better hurry up and piss off."

I realised I was embarrassed by Gary in front of the calmly sneering toe-rag, as if I had been taking the abuse in a manly way, more or less, until Gary came along and spoilt it with his prissy tale-telling.

"I bet you two spend fucking hours together in this poxy little shit-hole. I can't fucking imagine what you get up to."

"I'm sure you can't," retorted Gary.

"Don't get lonely here without us," the malevolent man-child continued; "we'll be back."

He ducked away. Then his voice came again, as if in afterthought.

"Oh, I think this is yours."

An object was hurled through the window and shattered against the far wall. Suddenly the kitchen was filled with a repulsive stench.

"Fuck," said Gary. "The little bastard's shat in a jar."

There were sounds of receding footsteps. Finding the kitchen oppressive, and not only because of the smell, I went to the front door. I paused, then grasped the latch and pushed it open. The continuous concrete balcony was empty. I felt immediate relief that was soon followed by tremors of some unidentifiable emotion containing anger, shame and obscure melancholy.

I closed the door again and turned to face Gary, who was now in the living room. I shook my head.

"Why the Doctor Who theme?" I asked.

"I don't know."

"Why did they call you a paedophile?"

"Fucking hell, what is this? They called you one, too. It wasn't just me."

"Sorry, I didn't mean it that way. I meant . . . What's the connection? Do you know them?"

"I don't know them."

The realisation that I had not used the chilli powder as I had planned hit me with a sense of sickening remorse. How weak I was. But then, I couldn't have—it was better that I hadn't. I felt empty, though, thinking about it. In retrospect—as, I now believed, during the recent encounter—I felt surges of unbearably bitter hatred alternating with surges of oven-hot love, the latter as if we had received some special attention that made me blush. Yet I felt ashamed and dirty, as if the idiotic crudities that had been directed at us had been composed of the most densely compressed insights about our inner natures that we were ever likely to meet. I wanted to shave off my beard. I couldn't help rubbing it now in discomfort and dismay.

Gary said he wanted to leave everything as it was until the police arrived, so we sat back down in our former positions. I felt that my soul had acquired a stain that could never be removed, and that it would not help, therefore, to talk about it. It was ridiculous anyway, to feel that way, yet the feeling was stubborn.

"They could have picked on anyone," said Gary, as if reading my thoughts.

"But what do you think that was all about? Don't you think there was something weird about the timing?"

"Not just the timing."

"Tell me, then. You've got a theory, haven't you?"

"Maybe more than one." He paused and took a breath as if assessing something. "But I'll give you one, for starters. What's the connection? That's what you asked, isn't it? Maybe that's the whole point— everything more and more connected. But connected with Direct Current. No gaps. No pause for reflection. No suspension. No . . ." He searched for the word. "No epoché. So, what if you do a search on Hamster Dam and this is registered with an algorithm? What if your name comes up again in a news story which is syndicated and put online? What if the same algorithm, according to its ever more refined specifications, sends that news story to the aggregate news feed of a group of anti-paedophile vigilantes?"

"If this were 2005, say, that would immediately strike me as a ludicrous paranoid fantasy."

"What about now?"

"Still speculative, of course, but . . . I don't know. Things have changed."

"Yes. In lots of ways."

I hung my head in thought.

"Gary," I said, "I believe you. The world is mad. The world is mad and we're charged with containing a few unfortunates . . . Well, never mind that. As you said, for the sake of trust itself, I believe you."

Gary was silent for a long time, his expression thoughtful, unreadable.

"Maybe that's the best I could hope for. I'm glad. It might already be too late for anything else, but I'm glad if you believe. That means you understand. That's what I wanted most, I think."

I nodded.

"I hope you don't forget." There was a strange inflection in his voice as he said this. It seemed to signify something but I could not say what. I thought he was going to pursue this chain of thought, but instead I was left waiting, as if someone had jumped off a diving board and no splash followed.

"Take me to the Grove," I said, breaking the silence.

"Yes." His voice was strangely distant. He nodded, then lifted his eyes to mine with a brief, but penetrating glance.

"We have to see the police first," he said wearily.

"Of course. Is anything wrong? What's on your mind?"

"Oh . . . well . . . nothing I haven't said before."

"You can say it again."

He smiled sadly. "The geeks have destroyed everything. Children sleep with their phones now. We've become so sick that we fight on the side of the exact people who want to abolish us. And it's already here. We've already lost. At least for the foreseeable future. And maybe forever. If we want to live now, at all, we have to go underground. Right, deep underground."

"Maybe," I said. "But we don't know that. Let's concentrate on preserving our possibilities. Anyway, we're alive. We don't have to ask anyone permission for that."

I sat up straighter, unnerved and determined not to nod off. Instead I turned my attention to the window. The scenery of streets, gardens, trackside trees, passed so quickly it was as if my eyes were constantly losing grip on it. But I tried to maintain that grip. I tried to understand what it is that we mean by 'mundane' when we refer to such sights. Something independent of our subjective experience. Yes, I knew this was important, and yet it kept slipping away from me.

Eventually I got home. The familiar domesticity seemed to break the hold of the phantasm that had been the unwelcome companion of my journey. Still, it was clear that I was suffering under some very unusual disturbance of mood. I splashed water on my face in the bathroom basin, made myself a cup of rooibos tea, and sat down on the sofa, trying to puzzle out exactly what had happened that day.

Something had happened, yes. Before the obvious event. Before, that is, the event that could be described even if it could not be entirely explained. So there had been two events, at least, and the second had followed closely on the first, so that I had not had time to consider what the first had really meant. I knew it had meant one thing, at least—that I now wanted to go with Gary to the Grove. But this time it had been Gary, not me, who had put off the visit.

I thought back on the first event, which had been linked in some way with our perusal of that strange website. If only I could get it all straight in my mind! I had told Gary that I believed him now, but did I? I had meant it when I said it. And anyway, believed what?

Obviously that was linked with the Grove—that was the point. But did I believe that the website had appeared because we had searched for Hamster Dam online? Or even, simply, because we had spoken about it? Or thought about it? That was fantastical enough, but suppose I did believe that—and perhaps I did—what else did that imply? Could I believe that *implication*? And the next one? I began to feel queasy as if I had agreed to scale a rock face without first examining it, and now stood at its foot, craning my neck, looking up.

But I had meant what I'd said. There was some key to it that I was forgetting now, I was sure. What was it? For the sake of trust itself! Yes, that was it. That was the key. Now I had to fit it in the right lock. But I couldn't find that lock. Trust. I repeated the word to myself. I knew it was a valid key. I knew I had used it before and it had worked. It would work again, therefore. I reassured myself on this point. I was tired now and I needed rest. Suddenly I remembered the horrible phantasm on the train. No, I couldn't go straight to bed. I would watch a comedy, take my mind off things. Then I would sleep. And I would contact Gary first thing in the morning and arrange our expedition to the Grove.

while I thought that I would have to go in to work, perhaps phoning and messaging Gary on my breaks. This pull, however, under these current circumstances, was not quite strong enough. I realised that I would have to put the mundane to one side. I would have to diverge from the course of the everyday and venture into the scrubland of the unusual. Already my blood was throbbing in my veins at the thought. It was not, of course, that my particular routine was empty of what most would consider unusual. For this escapade, however, I knew I would not be allowed the protective clothing of my professional role.

I read over the e-mail and printed it off, then I deleted it from my in-box. I recognised the quote at the end. As a matter of fact, I had seen it, again, just the night before. It was the first line of the poem by Julie that Gary had been trying to set to music some weeks back, 'The Discovery of the World'. Its theme had been uncharacteristically expansive for Julie, but, perhaps all the more for its grand subject matter, it was typical of Julie's productions in the impatience it displayed in sacrificing scansion to message and to a favoured image. The night before, the poem had still been on Gary's workbench where I had first seen it.

I folded the e-mail printout and slipped it into my jacket pocket. Then I mentally prepared myself to phone work and tell them that I was ill. I checked myself. Why should I lie? Surely I had legitimate reason to be concerned about Gary. Somehow, though, I had been infected by his sense of secrecy. I did not wish to treat this as a legitimate part of my job, though I might be forced to soon. As paranoid as his e-mail had sounded, I felt the instinct in me to honour its spirit by telling no one, for the moment, what I was about. I made the phone call, therefore, lying—necessarily or unnecessarily—that I had come down with food poisoning, and making—in an affected croaky voice—the required delegations.

It was with a rare sense of freedom—having finished the phone call and printed off a map of part of Burking Ryde—that I closed the door to my flat behind me and headed for the station. I had no idea how long this expedition would take, what it would involve or how it would end. In that sense, I might have been leaving the world itself, and I thought of how bounded our days usually are. But Gary had said he was "off to the world". A strange way of putting things. These thoughts led to other associations and speculations so that on the train I was hardly cognisant of my surroundings. I had an eerie sense that I was playing in reverse last night's troubled journey, but apart from that I sat tensely forward in anticipation of the nebulous unknown towards which I hurried. Again I tried to phone Gary and again received no answer. Again my text messages were sent out to an unresponsive blankness. The implications encoded in Gary's e-mail constricted with more biting reality each time my attempts to contact Gary failed.

Naturally, I went first to his flat. I had a vague memory, or pseudo-memory, that in situations such as this, feelings of anxiety subside as one approaches the location where one expects the missed or missing person to be. In this case, as I walked from the station along the semi-overgrown path to the Rimewell Estate, I was inexplicably stricken by a kind of emptiness resembling panic. Of course, I continued.

There was no answer when I pressed the door buzzer. It seemed likely, therefore, that there would be no use in me going up to the flat and knocking on the door, but I felt unable to leave the estate until I had done so. I pressed the buzzers of neighbouring flats until I managed to persuade someone to buzz me in. From the outside, Gary's flat seemed quiet and still. The boarded-up window showed that Gary had been active, as he had said he would, after I left. There were no signs of further damage, but I now noticed, written in black marker, graffiti in the same vein as the taunts we had endured from the roving vigilantes. I grimaced. I would not have wanted such things written on the outside wall of my flat. It seemed like they must taint the atmosphere within, that any exterior so befouled could not contain the easily breathable air of home. I had very little expectation, therefore, of an answer to my knock, but I was still disappointed when all I could detect within was hollow, unresponsive silence. The curtains were drawn, so I couldn't peer in through the unbroken windows. I was not sure I had ever seen the curtains drawn before. It seemed contrary to Gary's normal habits. I knocked again with the same result. Then I bent and looked through the letter-flap. The coffee table. Late morning gloom. Stillness. I had such a sense of emptiness at this scene that shivers ran down both my flanks.

I stood. With my back against the wall, I fished a small jotter from my pocket, tore out a page, wrote a quick message on it and posted it through the door. It was possible Gary's paranoia now extended to phones and that the note would therefore contain information that he had not yet seen—basically, my need to talk to him as soon as possible.

I was going to shout through the letter-flap before leaving, but somehow the thought of it made me shiver again and I turned away and left.

It was obvious where I should go next: that place to which Gary had first tried to take me and then had avoided taking me. It was time for me to visit the Grove.

Before leaving my flat I had done some preparatory research on the address Gary had given in his account of the library. There was a bus stop not far from the Rimewell Estate—I could take a bus from there, change once, and alight within ten minutes' walking distance from my destination. So I set out, trouble or perhaps exhilarated—as I had been earlier—by the feeling that this initiative of mine was entirely unauthorised. By whom? By Gary? By my employers? I could not quite say.

The daytime bus ride, on a workday, through the residential streets, town centres and leafy interstices of the outlying borough of Hintervale was a reminder of how little provision is made in our so-called civilisation for the solitary, though we are forced more and more to live apart from each other. The great emptiness of the weekday is avoided by huddling busily in the workplace. Then there are the other kinds of huddling to be done, at night or on the weekends, all as a means of ignoring the silence and emptiness that is the suffocating by-product of all this mindless huddling.

What happens, though, when a person is caught out, finds himself without distracting company and even, perhaps, without distracting gadgets? It is as if he is washed up on the comfortless kerbside. Life seems only as fertile and as sheltering as a grassy verge. He might easily find himself becoming one of those unfortunate, dubious people who stops strangers and asks for money. I had such thoughts as I looked out the bus window and the corners of roads angled by. At such moments it is very easy to feel one has wasted one's entire life. And yet another sensation begins to creep in, too, perhaps as frightening as the first—or more so. That is: it doesn't have to be like this. Things might still be changed. And now I began to believe I was gaining some inkling of how Gary had felt, suspended from work, cut off from his previous life by a cloud of suspicion, the future empty before him, convalescing indefinitely.

I alighted in a quiet commercial street, of what had once been a village—long since swallowed by the expansion of Greater London. On the other side of the road was a newsagent's with orange signage and large shop windows reaching close to the pavement. On this side of the road was an old red telephone box that looked like it might even contain a working telephone. I looked around to confirm the name of the street and to get my bearings by the turnings off. I could have used my phone for guidance, of course, but I didn't want to access anything that would request knowledge of my current location, although I supposed the mere presence of my phone on my person was sufficient for certain unknown parties to track me if they wished to.

What's more, I couldn't turn it off, in case Gary texted or made a call.

I considered, and I took the phone from my pocket and turned it off. I was on my own in a place I had never been to before, another obscure little patch of the world, of intersecting incidentals, either personal or impersonal, that were their own focus and did not need me for their continuation. There was uncertainty in what I was doing, but that was good.

I set out in what I judged was the right direction, at first going the way from which the bus had come but soon turning left down a street with houses on one side and a small green on the other. I realised there were few reminders—were there any? I didn't want to look too hard—in this area that we had entered the 21st century, whatever that might be. What was it, in fact? My uncertainty on this question increased the more I thought about it. I felt like whistling, and then, in fact, I did. It suddenly struck me that what had always cast a shadow of anxiety over my life was the future, and I laughed. This tree, at the corner of this garden here, just behind the red brick wall—a beech? I didn't know. Its leaves hung in the stillness of the day. What was time for this tree, for its surroundings? And yet the train on which I had come out, the flats and offices I had seen from its window, the phone I had just switched off, all this incredible infrastructure of electricity, metal, glass, plastic, information—all this was predicated on and strained towards a projected phantom of the future, and some people rose on the power of the dynamo thus created, and others fell. And I thought again of the half-overgrown path to the Rimewell Estate, and the spell, on one occasion, of its luxuriant silence, and I thought of buddleia growing at the sides of the railway track and of how peaceful they always seemed, with their drooping purple heads and their ragged masses of leaves. The glittering phantom of the future—how it enslaved us with the idea that we might be excluded from it. It was as if we had come to feel the future was more real than the present. We would be mocked and might lose our foothold in society if we did not believe in this phantom and dedicate our lives to it. That was what we now called reality, and we had lost even the faintest suspicion that we might be misusing the word.

Absorbed in such thoughts, examining the creased bark of a tree here, a cracked slab in the pavement there—now the bay window of a front room, now a scattering of brown juniper needles—I came sooner than I had expected and without difficulty to the double-gate beyond which lay the grounds of the library. There was no sign on the gate—closed and padlocked—to confirm the location, but Gary's description had been specific enough that there was little doubt I had arrived. No one seemed to be around. Should I simply scramble over the gates? I crossed the road to examine them more closely and realised it was unlikely I could climb over without sustaining an injury of some sort—probably on the elegant row of spikes at the top—if I managed it at all. Then I remembered that Gary had mentioned there was an easy way of getting over the wall. I began to follow the wall round to the left—as one faces the gate—in the hope of finding it. Since Gary had not said what the way was, I was not sure what I was looking for, or how easy he had meant by "easy". That was a word which, under the circumstances, might have meant anything short of impossible, or at least, I reasoned, anything up to 'not as hard as the gate'.

The wall was a few feet over head height, and trees had been planted close to it on the inside, for much of its circumference, long ago. The wall was obviously an old wall, too, its texture and materials varying along its length. Here and there, it was topped with broken glass embedded in cement—a preventative tactic that had fallen into disuse long ago. I looked for hand- and footholds in the outer wall, but for some time found nothing promising. Then I came to it. Could this be it? This section of the wall was constructed of stone in cement, and from below the middle of the wall a number of the stones had fallen away like rotten teeth, leaving only the cement's whitish gum.

I had no idea how quickly I could manage this, or if I could. I had no idea whether it was better to wait or to start immediately. Since I had no idea, I realised, the only question was one of nerves. Therefore, I took a breath, put my toe in one of the crevices, the fingers of my right hand in a higher crevice, and heaved myself up from the pavement. The first part of the operation was easy enough, but finding the next toe- and finger-holds was harder, especially as the task was to heave myself with these as the pivots of my strength and launch myself far enough over the top of the wall that only a minimal struggle would remain in order to haul my lower half up and swing my legs over to the other side.

Once I had begun this, I panicked, almost certain that someone would appear at the far corner and see me while I was in this helpless position. And in view of the report in the local paper of a strange man lurking about the area, they might be more than normally inclined to telephone the police.

For a moment of despair I thought I was going to lose strength and sink back down to the pavement, but my left foot found another toe-hold in good time and I pushed myself up onto the top of the wall, sitting up with my legs dangling above the library grounds. The height was a little daunting, but the longer I paused the worse it would be. I launched myself and the ground met me quickly enough, half-twisting my left ankle. I had also sustained a few scrapes and grazes in the climb, but the relief at being inside the wall and protected from the sight of strangers more than compensated for such minor distresses.

Now I had time to take in my surroundings. I realised I was not in a hurry. The Grove, anyway, had to be within these grounds, so it was a certainty that I was only moments away from it. Having said that, the grounds were unusually large and green for a library. A bed of roses off to the left bordered a tall hedge that presumably contained some feature of its own. To my right, trees dotted the lawn and a path wound between them—yew, horse chestnut and others. It struck me how hard it is to create a scene such as this—the blend of nature and culture, each merging into the other. Such a space always seemed inherited—beginningless, although to end it was trivially easy.

I went first to the rose bed. Crows marched singly up and down in haphazard lines. Their occasional caws seemed as if corresponding to the chimes of an ancient clock in a place where time is a very different matter. Strange that all this was locked up during the day, as if the roses and hedges and pathways and trees were all for the benefit of the crows and perhaps one or two currently invisible non-human denizens. The idea pleased me greatly for some reason. I looked around. The library building, now some distance to my left, rising greyish and stony beneath the overcast sky, was like some medicinal concentrate of the imaginative nutrients that made the lawns so emerald green, the trees branch with such a perfect realisation of déjà vu, the dense leaves of the hedge so heraldic. Think of it—to be a caretaker for such a place, dedicating the many pages filling the many rooms within, and the landscape miming contemplation through its flora and features without, to silence and clouds and falling wingnuts and the rhythms of non-human time. The very roses in front of me seemed to bloom, yellow and red, with some hint of the inky typeface of the supple-stiff printed leaves of the library shelves, as if all the black ribbing of script on white paper were some glorious eternal compost.

Charged, as it seemed, with the fecund meditation inherent in the garden itself, I decided there was nothing left to delay me, and I began to look about for the Grove. From Gary's description, it should have been by the wall. I moved towards the centre of the garden with the object of seeing more of the wall at one time. Widening my field of vision in this way, and turning repeatedly to stop and scan, I soon caught sight of something between the trees—an area of lighter green, shaped, but not with the clipped lines of the hedge—like something intended to conceal its own nature. Even if I had not suspected what it was, I believe I would have been intrigued. Now, I could not have chosen any other direction; I approached.

As I drew nearer, I saw the aperture that made a doorway. It was, from the exterior, as Gary had described. The bamboo canes formed a roughly oblong enclosure, the permeability of this screen allowing the most splintered glimpses of what was within, these glimpses exoticised by the elliptical leaves that obscured and interrupted in beautiful disarray like ruffled green feathers. For a moment I was convinced that the splinters of vision between leaves had indirectly disclosed to me the presence of life—human life—and a flame of excitement leapt up in me at the idea. However, as I drew closer still, I became doubtful, though the sense of strangeness and excitement did not entirely subside.

The doorway that was no more than a gap in the enclosing bamboo canes, grew more open and more revealing to me as my course became aligned with it. There was, I could now see, something to indicate that human life had been here, even if it was not here now. But why was the thought of human life so mysterious and exciting to me? Was it really human life I inferred from what I saw?

A few strides more and I was at the entrance to the Grove. The partial view I had had until this moment had prepared me only slightly for what I saw. In one sense I now grasped the meaning of what had before been merely suggestive, but in another sense I was confronted by a newly unavoidable confusion. The simplest way to describe what I saw is to say that it was a kind of sandcastle. However, both elements of that name would be misleading. It appeared to be made of dirt of some sort, but I don't believe it was the sand of the pit in which it had been built. There were bridges and other features that would not have held in place with normal sand, unless some kind of binding agent had been mixed in. Then again, the material did not look like cement to me, either. As to the 'castle' element of the description—perhaps 'citadel' would have been more appropriate. What was it, in fact? An answer came to me, but I did not understand it:

Hamster Dam.

But how could this be Hamster Dam?

For a while I merely stood in the entrance to the Grove and stared at it. Then, with what seemed to me appropriate caution and reverence, I stepped over the grassy threshold to examine it, hoping—longing, even—to understand.

Presumably, Gary had made this, although it looked more grown than made. I was reminded of the formations of a coral reef—not angular, but ramified in branches that, however rigid they might be, had rippled surfaces as if the result of pulsations that had solidified. The whole structure covered an area roughly twelve feet by six and did not overflow, at any point, the limits of the sandpit.

and beyond that, of tunnels and chambers populated by purposeful toy-beings, and beyond that, cellars and catacombs, and beyond that, a nebulous gateway made of the whole, remained intact, like a reality that had no need to consult my belief or disbelief. After several attempts at the assertion, I put aside such formalities. I continued to pace around this wonder of the unworld, to peer at windows, to stand back, stop and take it in at a certain angle. Looking at the paper snake hung between two lower turrets, at a rubber monster emerging from the arched mouth of a tunnel, at a plastic elven princess standing in strange companionship with a clockwork snail on a high rampart, I succumbed to a bewildered seizure of smiling—an involuntary, wordless admission of something. I remembered what Gary had said of the feeling of being in Hamster Dam—that it was happiness.

The monsters here were happiness, too. They were like guard dogs in a dream, whose very menace is your secret friend. Since this happiness was so palpable, and since, even in the middle of an overcast day, it seemed to lend the sand-acropolis-doll's-house a sunset glamour, since—also—this smile verging on laughter kept pulling tightly, of its own accord, at the ends of my mouth, I became convinced that part of this happiness was Gary's actual presence. Wasn't that what I had sensed when I had approached the Grove? And wasn't that a large part of my confusion when I had stood on its threshold? At some level, I had known he was here, and yet when I had looked around, he was nowhere, and there was nowhere he could hide. Now I looked away from the Dam and outward at the screening bamboo. Surely he was here? I was certain of it. I needed, but hardly dared, to call his name. My voice, anyway, spilled from my lips without any decision being made.

"Gary? Gary? Are you here? Can you hear me?"

I listened, and even believed that I was heard, even believed there was a response—a reply. It was silent. There were no words. But surely there had been a reply!

I stood looking and listening for some time, adjusting my position now and then as if I might see or hear what I was straining after if I faced a different direction. At first, I think, this activity was the expression of a feeling, as if I were theatrically projecting my sense of wonder outwards. However, something else crept in to the quality of my looking and listening. Rather than projecting, I became receptive. There was someone out in the grounds beyond the bamboo screen. I could hear something. Footsteps. Perhaps a cough. I could sense something in some indeterminate way—sense someone aware of my presence and setting their course for it.

I am not sure why, but I did not move towards the entrance of the Grove to see and to hail them. I stood where I was, listening, attentive, and waited.

There came a moment, with the unknown person within a few strides of the Grove's entrance, when my anticipation became unbearable. They must have been approaching at an angle, because I still could not see them. A different confusion than before was mixed in with this anticipation because the footsteps, as far as I could tell, did not belong to Gary. I felt unable to call out to verify this. I am not sure exactly what I was expecting—or perhaps I had not had exact expectations—but I know that I was tremendously relieved when a figure appeared in the opening between bamboo stalks and the range of possibilities folded like a fan into one actuality. Even with her before my eyes, a certain amount of puzzlement, anticipation and apprehension remained, but the suspense was deflated to bearable proportions. By deduction alone I might have guessed who it was, however, with Gary's description distinctly impressed in my memory, very little doubt remained.

I nodded. I could not quite think of her as a stranger, though it was possible or likely she knew nothing about my existence other than my presence in front of her.

"Hello," she said, remaining where she stood. "Are you looking for something?"

"Some*one*," I said. "Gary Weber, to be exact. You must be Miriam."

"Ah, I see you've heard of me. Are you a friend of Mr. Weber?"

"Yes. And workmate. As I said, I'm looking for him now. I haven't been able to get in touch with him, and—"

She began to walk over, but her eyes were on the Dam. She stopped in front of it, seeming to search it intently. Then she turned to me. "What's your name?" she said.

"Brian Warfield."

"I think I know something about you. I'm sorry. I knew about Gary, but he told me you were in his confidence. Also, I felt I shouldn't interfere."

"With what?"

She seemed about to reply, but remained silent for some time. Then she said, "What do you think has happened to Gary?"

It was my turn to struggle. Finally I said, "I don't know."

"Then that's my answer to you."

"I thought he was here," I said. "I mean, I thought you might be him. Have you seen him recently?"

"I saw him some days ago."

"And he was building this?"

"Yes."

"Did he say anything about his plans?"

"Yes. But I think he told me the same things he told you. There are two ways you can interpret what he said. You can believe it or not."

"Yes." I gritted my teeth and looked upward in exasperation, then I began to pace up and down by the side of the Dam. "Yes," I said. "And I thought I knew which it was."

When I looked at Miriam again, she held my eye, then she pointed, with steady hand, at the Dam.

"But it's impossible," I said.

I paced again, then stopped.

"Perhaps," I said, "perhaps you could talk to me for a while. I need to try and work this out."

She nodded.

"Shall we sit?" she suggested, and she indicated one of the benches facing the sandpit.

We sat down almost in unison (next to each other). I stayed silent for some time, with my elbows on my knees and my left fist wrapped by my right hand pressed against my mouth. There was only one thing to talk about. At last I found my voice.

"Belief—that's the crux of it. As you've pointed out. Well, let's suppose that I believe, and put aside for the moment the question of what exactly, I still don't know whether to think it's wonderful or terrible."

Miriam did not reply to this and it occurred to me that I had not actually asked a question.

"All right," I said, "here's something. I'm supposed to believe—I know that's what Gary wanted from me—but it seems like you already did believe. Is that true? Why did he need me to believe, too?"

"I think I can answer that," she said. "That is, I know why, but I'm not sure what I say will make sense to you."

"Go on. I want to hear."

"It might be a bit of a long story, but I don't think I've ever had the chance to tell it, so, well, at least I'll be doing as you asked and talking to you for a while."

"I would appreciate it. Maybe it's better for me to listen for a while, too."

"I did believe Gary, yes. In some sense that helped him, but not in exactly the sense he needed. You see, I think I am part of what he wanted you to believe in."

"You're not real?"

She smiled and laughed faintly.

"Funnily enough, I'm not sure that I am, not in the sense I think you mean. I am not sure that I ever was. I have never had a strong sense of reality—of belonging to what other people call reality, I mean.

"When I was eleven years old, I made a single decision that affected the rest of my life. I noticed that people decided to believe that bad things were more real than good things. This is what they called 'living in reality'. Almost everyone made this decision, because almost everyone before them had made the same decision. It was a question of numbers—always a question of numbers. And the effect this decision had, of almost everyone believing bad things are more real than good things, was, and is, to make the world a very bad place. People believe that the only important thing is to fight to take their place—in society or history or whatever it might be—and even if they were first naturally inclined to do good, because they decided to believe good was less real, they find bad more persuasive and they give in to it, for the sake of power and prominence, and so they perpetuate the cycle. Bad becomes more pervasive, and so it becomes more persuasive.

"I saw all this, in my own particular way, when I was eleven, and I knew that I wasn't an extravagant heroic type, but I knew also that, for the sake of my soul, I had to resist this influence that held sway in the world and which turned life into a strange silence, since the truth was a hidden, unspoken thing because of it—so I made a very solemn decision that I would never believe in what other people called 'reality' but only in good. And I knew that, in order to live by this decision, I had to become a reader. Wait, I shall tell you what I mean by that.

"What I don't mean is that I decided I had to study in order to master some sort of battle skill. Perhaps I'm not explaining myself well. It wasn't that I wanted to conquer fields of knowledge or develop some kind of mental jiu jutsu. There's nothing wrong with knowledge, of course—I had to study to qualify as a librarian—but that wasn't the meaning, for me, of being a reader. What the meaning was, was to be a kind of custodian for the silence I was talking about—the silence pushed into the background by everyone believing bad is more real than good. I've always thought another word for this silence is 'obscurity'. The root of the word is 'darkness', of course, but we don't mean 'darkness' in conversation, do we? We usually mean the opposite of fame. Like invisibility. Well, I think even famous people can be covered in obscurity. Things can be invisible to the mind even when they are not invisible to the eyes. That's not exactly what I mean, either, but maybe it'll become clearer as I go along.

"I discovered there was something particular about books—mainly fiction, poetry and memoir, but other kinds of book, too. But you could not find this thing— this obscurity—in other *forms* of printed matter, like magazines and newspapers, and you certainly can't find it on the internet. And that thing was the obscurity I'm talking about. When you spend time with it, the need to fight for a position dissolves. There are always only two souls, or only as many as can bear the intimacy without breaking it, involved. But the connection of two souls is the pattern for the intimacy. The writing and the reader, or maybe the book and the reader. Each book has its particular silence, its particular obscurity. You might think silence and obscurity is all the same. In a way that's true, but read a book, really read it, and you'll understand the true richness of that obscurity, because it can hold something so particular, and not just one thing, but countless particular things. And that's exactly what the particular is for—to demonstrate this richness in obscurity.

"I know you think I'm contradicting myself, but I'm trying to be as true as I can to something that is always shifting even though it is always the same.

"Anyway, the decision I made was to be a guardian of every secret silence banished to the pages of a book.

"I'll tell you a story that might help. I found it in a book called *The Details of Time*, which is a collection of interviews with someone called Ernst Jünger. At one point Jünger talks of his meeting with Picasso. He says he was in Picasso's studio and Picasso turned one of his newly finished paintings to face the wall. He said to Jünger, 'I'm going to leave it like that so no one can see it. You're probably wondering why. It's because even if no one sees it, a painting makes a difference to the universe.' And that is the spirit in which I have read books. Even if the reading only exists in my own mind, it makes a difference to the universe.

"People have very strange ideas about books. As a reader—the kind of reader I've always tried to be—and as a librarian, I've come to understand that there's a chasm between what people think books are and what they truly are. For one thing, people think that if you've had a book published you must be famous. But I've known some very, very dusty books in my time and it seems to me that a book is really more a route to obscurity than to fame. This gets a bit complicated, because in our world it's everything that's most valuable and important that's obscure. And so, in a sense, not only are books a route to obscurity, but they're meant to be. In the world and the age that we live in, if a person starts, say, with a fame balance of zero when they're born, all else being equal, writing a book will take them below zero. It makes them positively esoteric, because it takes them into a world where people have to wake up and think and make an effort. On the other hand, if the same person just goes about their normal life these days, and posts a video or two of themselves washing their cat or singing karaoke on the internet, the credit in their fame account will soar. They will be part of the consciousness of hundreds of thousands of other humans instantaneously. So the real achievement is obscurity, you see.

"Anyway, because that's what I've devoted my life to, I could tell, when I first spoke to Gary, that his destination was very similar, and I knew the library grounds were exactly the haven he needed.

"But because I am, in some way, part of his destination, he couldn't build a bridge between me and there. He needed someone else."

By now it was useless to remark that this was all very strange. I checked myself.

"But he wanted to build the bridge from me?"

"Yes. You must realise that. After all, you see, I was in his dream—as the hare. I don't know exactly what that bodes for me. I have a funny feeling about it. He wasn't going to tell me at first, you know. He was afraid that I wouldn't be the person he believed I was."

"But he found out you were?"

"He talked to me and, yes, he was satisfied I was the person."

I thought, my eyes directed at the tips of my shoes as if they were some measure of reality. I could not tell whether there was any use in thinking about the matter further.

"This is all very . . . wonderful," I said.

Clearly Miriam could tell I was perplexed. She patted my shoulder.

"But," I said, "what if he is somewhere else, in need of help?"

"Where else do you think he might be?"

"I don't know."

"If you think there's somewhere he might be, obviously you should go there."

"But you don't think he's anywhere else?"

"No. Nowhere that we can reach him. Or not yet."

"No. Nor do I."

For a while there was silence, then I got to my feet and began to walk once more around the Dam. The stairways and bridges, the ramparts in layered perspective, the beautiful, childish pennants above, waiting to flutter in some promised wind not of this world. Everything suggested that we had caught the Dam frozen for a moment in the middle of its own life. How could Gary be anywhere but here, if, indeed, he was anywhere in the world at all? I stopped and bent a little and reached forward to touch the round wall of a corner tower. I hesitated with my fingertips centimetres away, and then I touched it. Cold, just like concrete. Yet there was a strange thrill to its solidarity. Could it really be so hard? It glittered a little, as if varnished, and I even thought for a moment that this surface was like the scales of a living creature.

Despite everything, again, I smiled. It was inexplicable.

Finally, I returned to the bench. I was in no hurry to leave. Whatever I was returning to it now seemed less real than this, and so could wait.

We talked for some while longer. Miriam confirmed in more detail what Gary had told me of the plans to convert the library into some kind of health club. I felt a little as if I were hearing that a man with a terminal disease was to have his hand amputated when he had only days to live. It seemed nonsensical and I couldn't quite concentrate my mind on it. I gave my contact details to Miriam and she gave me hers. Still we continued to talk, and the conversation entered strange and difficult territory whose contours I find I have no reason to record here. Eventually, Miriam said she had to leave and offered to escort me from the grounds so that I didn't need to climb back over the wall. I wanted to be left alone awhile with the Dam and my thoughts, but then again, I was afraid of being alone now in this place of unanswerable wonder. I saw in the lengthening shadows a loneliness and amazement greater than I had known before, and I accepted Miriam's offer without voicing my thoughts.

It was peculiar to have the gates locked behind us and to go our separate ways. I wandered for a while dazedly without thinking of destination, then a thought occurred to me—I switched my phone on again. There were no messages. This absence caused a terrible pang in me. I realised I was not sure how to get back to the place where I had alighted from the bus, but I felt a desperate urge now to return once more to Gary's flat, simultaneous with the dread of finding—as I fully expected—that it was still empty. In this terrible confusion of feeling, I painstakingly retraced my steps to the library, and from there—battling the allure of, or retreating in dread from, those enclosed grounds— worked out the route I had taken to arrive at the library in the first place.

After much dreary frustration and the particular agony that comes with impatience for a thing I did not believe would manifest, I made it back to Gary's flat. Of course, there was no response from within to my knocking on the door. Repeated texts and attempts to phone were all thwarted by the invincible void at which they were apparently aimed.

I sat down outside the flat with my back to the wall. How long would I wait? I grew cold. Unanswerable questions kept gnawing at me. There was no one even to keep me company in my suspense, so that I might feel this desert of uncertainty had its bounds and limits and that, however its existence might appal me, I could return from it to my native country.

I think I had not sat there for an hour yet when I was seized by another urge. Why had I come back here to the flat? Why had I passed the grounds of the library by? I had to return there on my own.

The journey was, in its way, even worse than the journey from the library grounds to the Rimewell

VII: Electric Dream

I saw very clearly that everything was my fault—that ruin had come because I was flawed. I had tried, all along, to do the right thing, and yet, at every point of the process there had been vacillations, and the wrong motives had entered in each time and disguised themselves as the right motives. When I understood this, I became "fuzzy", to use Gary's word—fuzzy through and through.

My life has changed. I never could have anticipated such a change. Most of my energy now is given over to means of maximising secrecy. Obscurity has become an urgent matter for me, like air. I will probably never type this up, and I shall be very careful who I show it to.

Gary was never found, and I have a very particular reason for believing he never will be. I have to remember what he said about the end of time—otherwise it is too horrible. I don't know, either, what has happened to Miriam. I did not try to contact her immediately after that day. I think I really went mad, and it has been very hard for me to claw my way back to sanity, but I have just about managed it. Carefully, carefully, with much agony and with moments of wrenching effort, I have pieced together what happened and what sanity is. In fact, I am not sure that I *return* to sanity; unless I had it and lost sight of it as a child, I am now coming to it for the first time. Either way, it is a rare and difficult thing to uncover.

It is hard to think of the future. I think of obscurity instead. I must perfect the ways in which the in between things that Gary spoke of can survive. Everything else is secondary.

It is hard to know what I would have concluded if I had done no further investigation and had not, therefore, looked again at the Hamster Dam website. I was already beyond skepticism when I returned to the Grove, but I think the uncertainties of the situation might still have allowed me to put certain questions aside. I would have been altered, haunted, but I am not sure I would have been propelled into a different mode of life entirely. That is my guess, but it was, anyway, inevitable that I would do as I did, inevitable that, in order to learn more about Hamster Dam, I would revisit one of the only sources known to me.

My first shock came simply when I entered the words "Hamster Dam" into Google and clicked on "search". How long had it been since I had last done this, with Gary? A week? I am not sure now, but it can't have been much longer. I expected, as before, that there would be a single relevant result and nothing to search through. In fact, there was now at least two screens of relevant results—I did not look further—and the website that Gary had shown me was not the first among them. The top result, in fact, was a discussion thread at Reddit. There were a smattering of similar threads at different sites. Kalpa Online had an article—'Raiders of the Lost Dam'—that talked of the strange recoveries being made online of what had been entirely forgotten areas of pop culture. Hamster Dam was the example with which the article opened. Other examples were given. The tone of the article gave me a strange frisson. It was a kind of fascination—of course, that was what such articles were for—but what was the real cause of this fascination? It seemed to achieve its most undiluted form when the author dwelt on some examples of recovered pop culture whose original, pre-internet existence seemed doubtful. It was, the article said, "part of the nature of the internet that it flattens the reality of those things that it catalogues. When Wikipedia entries are flagged for questionable notability, it is other internet citations, not citations of printed matter, that are required to bring the entries in line, or into legitimate reality. So the internet becomes self-referential and, with copypasta, memes and the wholesale disregard of authorship, authentication and so on, who is to say, in the end, that these 'recovered' shows, too—perhaps faked or falsely remembered—won't become as real as the others? Our dreams, our memories, our jokes and our lies might become one authorless and open-source Wikipedia, forever updating itself, forever quibbling between versions, with all the original means of judging between the authenticity of one version and another lost forever."

Reading the article through to the end, I was unable to tell whether the author was lamenting this state of affairs or celebrating it. I even began to suspect, though I was not sure, that there was some joke or hoax behind the article itself. A meta-joke, I suppose.

I looked through other articles and message boards. An indescribable choking sensation made it hard for me to linger on any of them for very long. At last I returned to the site that Gary had shown me. I wanted to find the site owner's e-mail address and try to compose a coherent message to him asking what he knew about the origins of Hamster Dam. I did write such an e-mail, though not till much later, and perhaps not coherently. When I eventually wrote, I received no reply. Something stopped me from carrying out my intention the first time. As I said, I was looking for an e-mail address. The site had expanded considerably in the brief time since I had first seen it, and somehow, during my exploration, I clicked on a link to a novelty image gallery, separate to those with representative stills from the series. A paragraph of text above the images in this newly added gallery explained what was displayed beneath. Recently Google had released the results of what had happened when images had been fed into their image recognition program and put into a feedback loop so that the recognised features were emphasised. Later I saw the original results of this process—strange, digital landscapes with celestial pagodas melting into mountains and lakes, a doughnut like a two-headed sea slug on a napkin of swirling arabesques, and so on. Someone with access to this program, seemingly intrigued by the 'recovered' children's show Hamster Dam, had put some of the stills from the website through the same process, and these formed the gallery on whose thumbnails I now clicked.

It is true, though unsatisfying, to say that I cannot describe them, or at least, I cannot describe what was most significant about them, and even a bare physical description is difficult. For instance, in the first one I clicked on, the raw material for which had been a wide-screen shot of Hamster Dam Village, wormholes had opened in the sky between the windmills, from which there seemed to spread to the rest of the picture a distinctly wormy influence. The sails of the windmills were something like flies' wings and appendages seemed to flicker from beneath the eaves of roofs like the limbs of funnel-web spiders lurking at the doors to their burrows.

There were perhaps six or seven pictures in all. The second one was stranger than the first, and the third stranger than that. These were supposed to be the dreams of the rudimentary AI program used in image recognition. What was the subtext in which they were passed on and displayed like this? Was it, perhaps, some version of this thought?: "Look, everyone, it's working. Our science has given dreams to the great, sleeping machine, and whatever is dreaming will eventually awake. Watch, now! Watch how quickly the dreams form, how furiously they elaborate themselves, with what alien combinations of colour, like the nightmares of a cuttlefish. Watch, and wonder how long is left to sit and watch and wonder. Watch, if you wish to catch some glimpse in this embryo of the future waiting to be born."

With a kind of moral repugnance then, an unwelcome sense of uncanny possibilities for which no defence had been prepared, I progressed from one image to the next. It was when I came to the fourth of these images that I realised nightmare was not only suspension, or some endlessly deferred menace. The air pressure in the room seemed to change in moments as if I had suddenly been dropped into a bottomless void. The original picture, before its treatment, had been Blue Boy crashing his biplane into the riverbank. What had once presumably been Blue Boy was now crawling from the wreckage. It gave the impression of escaping, surviving, at a terrible cost. Smoke billowed into the sky and from it were born post-human obscenities of all kinds—of kinds not yet enumerated. A little stronger, perhaps, than a watermark, a meta-pattern emerging from these patterns, was a face, with eyes and mouth wide open. There was no mistaking who it was—I wish there had been. It was Gary—trapped, woebegone, his face as if frozen alive, contorted with the agony of doom that was the last of all human life.

Milton Keynes UK
Ingram Content Group UK Ltd.
UKHW030925040924
447871UK00005B/117